This Is Where It Gets Interesting

Stories

John H. Matthews

*Acknowledgment is made to the
following, in whose pages these stories first appeared:*

*2ND Hand, Cellstories, Denver Syntax, Empty Headed: a
Literary Magazine, Opium Magazine, Pequin, Pindeldyboz,
Prairie Light Review, Still in Spin, Strong Coffee, The
Whirligig, Wisconsin Review, Umbrella Factory, Word Riot.*

ISBN: 0615644759
ISBN 13: 9780615644752
LCCN: 2013920947
Six Slug Books
P. O. Box 804688
Chicago, IL 60680
www.sixslug.com

For Rachel
and
For my parents

Contents

Odds

I went into a restaurant and sat at a long white counter. The cook took my order: a Reuben with fries. I didn't know where the waitress was.

It was six o'clock on Monday night. I'd closed up at the office and come here. I would check the race results when I got back to the apartment, maybe make myself a scotch and soda and forget about everything.

I'm a statistician. I compile odds and give them to people who need them: insurance companies, law firms, businesses. I take everything into account, and then I tell them the numbers and what they mean. You see, most people look at numbers and they have no idea, especially with statistics. It's all in the way you look at it. One way might tell a certain story; another way, the story might be completely different— like what's said about planes being safer than cars. Sure, there are fewer plane-related deaths every year, but there are also a hell of a lot fewer planes than cars, which changes the meaning of the numbers entirely. Anyway, that's what I do. It's work that's a lot like trying to stick a struggling worm on a hook.

As I waited for my food, I was writing numbers on a piece of paper in front of me in a long column. I was deducting from a thousand.

An attractive woman came in and sat next to me. She asked what I was doing.

"Nothing important," I said.

"Would you mind doing something for me, then?" she asked.

"Sure," I said.

"How about giving me a light?"

I took my Zippo from my coat pocket and really looked at this woman. She was young, maybe twenty-seven, had her hair done up nicely, wore red lipstick and a green business outfit, and had good legs. I got all this immediately. I lit her cigarette—a Lucky Strike. I noticed that too. I gave myself three-to-one odds that I'd get her number. I didn't go further than that. Nothing is a certainty. Just because you drop a dime a thousand times and it falls to the ground doesn't mean that it's going to do the same thing on the thousandth-and-first.

"Thanks," she said. She picked up the menu and scanned it professionally. The cook came with my plate, and she ordered a club sandwich and coffee. As I was putting down the meal, she grabbed my list of numbers.

"Declining increments of twenty-three," she said.

"Yes."

"Why?"

"It's a concentration exercise," I said.

"That's a strange thing to do."

"Not really."

"Does it help?"

"Sure, I guess."

"What do you need to concentrate about?" she asked.

"The future."

"Don't we all?" she said, laughing. "What's your line of work?"

"Odds," I said. "I'm a statistician."

The woman smiled to herself. Her club sandwich arrived.

"My late husband died in a railroad accident." she said. "What are the chances of that?"

"It depends."

"On what?"

"On how much you believe accidents are really accidents."

"It was an accident," she said, "just like any other kind."

"*Double Indemnity*," I said.

The woman laughed.

"Sorry," she said, "bad joke. I made that up about my husband. He died of natural causes; his heart stopped."

"Too bad," I said, thinking: *Heart disease is the number one killer of American males.*

"I'm sorry I'm so morbid," the woman said, extending a hand. "I'm Dana."

"Good to meet you, Dana," I said. "Ralph Seibold."

"Busy tonight, Ralph?"

"I've got a date with a TV set," I said.

"Break it. I'm a lot more exciting."

"I'll bet you are." I asked for a refill on my coffee.

"I'm just back from Europe," Dana told me. "France. First time."

"Know the language?"

"A woman doesn't need to."

"Touché."

"Actually, I do know a little. My late husband taught me some. He knew six languages."

"A professor?"

"Yes, for a time. Frightfully boring. I was just a China doll he liked to take out to cocktail parties and show off."

"I'm sorry."

"Make it up to me, then."

"How?"

"There's a drive-in not far from here, isn't there? Let's go see something."

"All right," I said.

I got the bill and paid it. Together, it came to six-fifty.

We parked in front of *Godzilla vs. the Smog Monster*. Dana said she wanted to see a movie where she wouldn't have to concentrate. I spread a blanket out on the hood of the Malibu, and she munched away on the hot buttered while Godzilla breathed fire. So far, I knew nothing about Dana except her name and that she had a dead husband. I decided to find out more.

"Dana," I said, "why are we here?"

"We're having fun, silly."

"Nothing else?"

"Of course, nothing else. Really, do you think I murdered my husband?"

I shook my head.

"All right. Here, have some popcorn. Cheer up." She gave me a nudge with her knee.

"Did you get that tan in France?" I asked.

"No," she said, "about six blocks away at Brenda's Tanning Salon."

"Oh."

During the movie, I spent the time trying to figure something out. It was that way with me—always playing it around, always looking at the angles.

"How long has he been dead?" I asked Dana, once we'd started on the way back.

Dana looked down at her watch.

"I'd put it at six hours," she said.

I nearly swerved off the road. Instead, I slammed on the brakes, sending gravel all through the tire wells and into the grass.

"Relax," Dana said soothingly. "It really was natural causes. I'm out celebrating."

"Jesus!" I said. Dana passed me a cigarette, which she apparently saw that I needed. I got the car moving again.

"That was a good movie," she said.

"Was it?"

"No, but I'm in such a good mood, it was anyway."

"Why is that?"

"Because I'm a rich widow now. I guess it was wish fulfillment."

"He doesn't sound like he was a great prize. Why did you marry him?" I said, watching the curl of blue cigarette smoke.

"Why does anybody? You're young and stupid. It doesn't have a lot to do with the person. It's the timing."

"Why didn't you divorce him?"

"It would have been inconvenient. Besides, we had an open relationship."

"And now?" I asked.

"And now I'm a widow riding in a car with a statistician."

"This is a good time for you?"

"As good a time as any, I guess."

"Did you find the body?"

"The maid did. She called me and I rushed over. I played the grieving wife and all that."

"Are you?"

"Am I what?"

"Grieving."

"I just told you, I'm happy."

"Strange emotion under the circumstances, even if you didn't like him."

"Not as strange as deducting twenty-three from a thousand."

"All right," I said.

"All right, what?"

"I'm taking you home."

"You honestly think I'm a killer?" Dana looked out the window, offended.

"No, I think I'm going to take you to bed."

"What makes you so sure I like you?"

"When you came back from the bathroom, you'd redone your makeup."

"Women do that."

"They also send their husbands to early graves."

"He was fifty-seven."

"Fifty-seven varieties of dead?"

"That's not funny."

"Sorry."

"Hey, how about a drink?" Dana said. We were coming up on a small roadside bar.

"All right."

I pulled in. It was a quiet, rustic place: wood floor and bar, moose head on the wall, candles. We took a table in the back, and I got us a couple of gin and tonics.

"I'll be right back," I said, placing the glasses down.

"Where are you going?"

"I'm going to call my bookie and see how the horses ran."

"Hurry back."

When I returned, Dana was examining a print on the wall.

"Houdini, eh?" I said.

"He was a great escape artist," she said.

"Are you?"

"Why are you so sure I killed my husband?"

"Because."

"Because, why?"

"Because I called your maid and told her I was the chief of police and you'd already confessed."

"Funny."

"Actually, Elita said you didn't have a husband at all."

Dana went slightly pale.

"How did you get the number?"

"There aren't many people in Grass Valley named Trembly."

"How did you find that out?"

"I asked the bartender. You made eye contact with him when we came in."

"You'd have made a good detective," Dana said sourly.

"Too late."

We sipped our drinks. Dana pulled self-consciously at her sleeve.

"So, is that exciting?" I asked after a couple of minutes.

"What?"

"Playing the rich widow?"

"Sometimes."

"Only six hours dead! Do your other pickups like that?"

"Sure. Everybody likes a little twist."

"Well, what if I told you I'm going to go home now and watch TV until I fall asleep?"

"You won't."

"How much would you bet?"

"Forget it," she said, darting to her feet. "You probably count the strokes, anyhow."

"You forgot your purse," I said.

Dana came back, snatched it up, and slammed out the door. The bartender mopped the bar with a rag and I laughed. I was up fifty on the ponies. I was happy. I didn't need to get into the sack with a stranger, not tonight.

I brought out my little list of numbers again, took a long drink, and started counting down.

The Black Tornado

E d Skimmington sat in the alley behind Holt's Gym, puffing on a cigarette and staring at shards of broken glass. His gorilla mask lay beside him on top of a yellow sign that said "50% OFF." He was thinking about his father, a man he had never quite forgiven for abandoning his mother when he was six years old.

He was on lunch, technically, though he rarely ate lunch—or much else really—preferring to spend his time with his cancer sticks away from public view. Getting in and out of the gorilla costume took about fifteen minutes and just wasn't worth the trouble. He was too lazy to pack lunches.

A strange wind came up suddenly and created a small black tornado inside the alleyway. It picked up random bits of newspaper, Popsicle sticks, alleyway grit, and glass.

Ed wondered at the manifestation. It had all the qualities of a real tornado—the funnel shape, the rotating winds—but this tornado was only about six meters tall and didn't threaten to do much damage.

He briefly considered going inside the gym and calling someone to witness this thing, but he figured that the wind burst would be gone by the time he got back, and anyone he brought outside would just think he was crazy. There were already too many people who thought he was crazy.

Ed continued smoking his cigarette as he watched the tornado do its erratic dance. Five minutes later, he was damned if the thing wasn't still going. It had changed positions numerous times but had never moved more than ten meters away from him.

It was certainly odd, in a *Ripley's Believe It or Not!* sort of way. From where he sat, sucking on yet another Pall Mall, Ed couldn't even feel a slight breeze. The weather was mild—a sunny October day in the mid-sixties, not a cloud in the sky. There seemed to be no explanation for the thing. It was weird, but not unbelievable. There were a lot of things Ed didn't, and never would, understand. Thirty-six years of living had proven that. If he couldn't understand how simple appliances worked, how was he going to explain this? He wasn't.

When Ed had finished off his third cigarette and his lunch break was over, he stood up and flicked the butt into the still-spinning tornado. Greedily, the tornado added this new item to its mix and sent it spinning around its self-contained universe. Ed picked up the mask and sign and started walking around to the front of the gym. At the mouth of the alley, just before he donned the humid mask, he noticed that the tornado had moved with him.

"What the shit?" Ed muttered.

Ed went a few more steps and watched in amazement as the twister followed.

"Jesus Christ on a cracker."

He made a tentative aggressive motion with the "50% OFF" sign, and the tornado rolled back. He could have sworn it did a little dip and bob and feigned a punch of its own, like a boxer.

Shaking his head, Ed put the ape mask back on and proceeded around to the front of the gym. It was probably the lack of oxygen in the mask; he was light-headed from wearing it all day and then smoking too many cigarettes in rapid succession. When he was resituated between a parking meter and an abused-looking sapling, Ed started waving at traffic and shaking the yellow sign.

People on the street started honking at him—honking more than usual, it seemed. A few minutes later, Ed noticed that the twister had followed him to the front of the gym and was quietly buzzing a short distance from him.

Foot traffic stopped as people gawked and gasped at the ape-man and the fantastic little black tornado. Children whooped with delight, thinking maybe the tornado was some Disney character invention they hadn't yet heard of. Others went by giving the pair a wide berth, as you would a ladder offering bad luck.

One young man stopped and scratched his goatee.

"How do you do that?"

"How do I do what?"

"How are you making that thing go?"

"I'm not," Ed said, shaking the sign. "Time to get in shape! Fifty percent off on the first three months of membership!"

The young man laughed. "Ah, a magician never reveals his secret, huh?"

"What can I tell you?" Ed said.

The man shook his head and walked off laughing. "Good trick . . . good trick."

The tornado prompted similar reactions from other pedestrians. Some pointed, others clapped. Everyone wanted to know what was causing it. Ed, however, continued to extol the virtues of fitness, acting as if the tornado wasn't there at all. It was slightly worrisome, though, this thing. Ed wondered whether the dancing tornado might not be a manifestation of the Grim Reaper or something, letting him know it was all going to be over soon. But if that was the case, why didn't the thing just strike and get it over with? It didn't seem malicious, but Ed watched it closely through the eyeholes just the same.

It wasn't long before the inevitable happened: Aaron, Ed's manager, came flying out the door of the gym. He put his hands on his athletic waist.

"What the hell is that?" he demanded.

Ed shrugged. "It was in the alley when I was on lunch, and now it's out here."

Aaron looked up at the sky. He wetted his finger and tried to feel a breeze.

"Come on Ed, what's the gimmick?" he asked.

"Hell if I know," Ed said. "Sunspots or something."

Noting the amount of attention the tornado was generating, Aaron's face cracked into a smile, but it then quickly fell into a frown.

"Is it dangerous?" he asked. "The last thing we need is a lawsuit."

"I'm not sure," Ed said. "It seems harmless."

"Hmmm . . . OK, well, keep it to the side so it doesn't impede foot traffic. It's a good trick, Ed, but your pay rate's gonna stay the same."

"Whatever."

As Aaron went back into the store, several people saw him get flipped off by a gorilla.

Two hours later, the tornado was still spinning and dancing, and Ed was about to come off shift. Several times, when no one was around, he had tried to talk to the tornado—thinking maybe it was a supernatural manifestation, like a ghost or something—but none of his attempts had elicited any response. Still, the thing seemed to have a personality.

At three o'clock sharp, Ed stopped waving to people and started walking toward the alley. He'd been instructed by Aaron on his first day of work that he should never remove the ape mask in front of the public. Aaron had said some bullshit about "ruining the illusion" or something, but Ed knew his boss just didn't want the populace to see his haggard, whipped mug—especially when the gorilla icon was supposed to be about robust fitness.

Ed returned to the alley and the twister followed him like a puppy dog. As it dragged along behind him, the tornado picked up more trash and whirred at an accelerated rate. He opened up the back door to the gym, and the twister rushed up and blew the door open wide as it followed him in.

"OK, that's enough, now," Ed scolded. "Go home already."

But the tornado only wiggled.

Several gym members looked up from their machines. Ed quickly walked off the floor and into the locker room to get out of sight. He removed the gorilla costume, hung it up in a closet, and put his street clothes back on. The twister remained at his side the whole time.

It was also there when Ed went to get his day's pay from Aaron, who told him to knock it off already; the joke was old.

"Don't come back here with that nonsense tomorrow," he said. "Tornadoes don't sell memberships."

Ed stuffed the cash into the front of his slacks and left quickly before all of Aaron's paper work got blown around the office. Luckily, he lived close by and didn't need to take public transportation; he figured that, under the circumstances, it wouldn't have worked out too well.

En route to his apartment, he stopped off at Angelo's for a couple of red hots and a handful of greasy fries, a combo that always managed to turn the bottom of the brown bag a translucent color.

Several customers ran in horror, crossing themselves as they went, shouting "*Diablo! Diablo!*"

"What the fuck is that?" Chet, the fry cook said.

"It's my pet tornado," Ed said. "The parrot didn't work out."

"Shit," Chet said. "Does it clean homes? My old lady doesn't even know what a dust rag looks like."

"I dunno," Ed said. "It doesn't seem to do much."

After Ed got his order, he decided to take a slightly different route home, one that would enable him to cut some distance through a park, where the tornado might attract less notice. He only hoped that he didn't come across any dog leavings—he was already being trailed by a funnel of Styrofoam cups, beer labels, newspapers, and a fine grey dust composed of God-knows-what.

When Ed came to a park bench, he decided to eat dinner there. As he lunged for a Vienna, the tornado cleared its throat.

"That shit's gonna kill you," it said.

Ed jumped and almost dropped his dog. Mustard dripped onto his pants.

"*What?*"

"Alcohol, cigarettes, and hot dogs," the tornado said. "That's not very healthy."

Ed bit defiantly into his hot dog. He was damned hungry.

"What the hell are you?" he said around a mouthful.

"I am from beyond," the tornado said.

"Well, you can go back," Ed said, unimpressed. "You're nothing but trouble."

"I wish it were that easy," the tornado said.

"Look, I don't need to hear *your* problems," Ed said. "I got enough of my own."

"Ed, we need to talk," the tornado said.

"We *are* talking."

"No, I mean really have a heart to heart. This is serious."

Ed sighed and rubbed his eyes. "Christ. Can this wait until after I get some beers in me?"

"By all means," the tornado said.

"Fine. And if I talk to you, will you leave me alone?"

"Hopefully."

That sounded good enough to Ed. He balled up his food wrappings and tossed them into the swirling winds. "Let's hit it," he said.

It was four blocks to Denizen's, a bar where Ed had a reputation for spending most of his evening hours. Lorraine, the owner, was an angelic, aging pinup beauty. She was working behind the counter when Ed came in and took a seat mid-bar.

Several patrons leapt back at the sight of the black tornado. Ed's assertions that it was harmless went unheard; even Lorraine was frightened. Only Mickey, the Vietnam vet, seemed unconcerned.

"Ed, I can't serve you with that thing in here," Lorraine said.

Ed protested, but it was no use. While he was hashing it out with Lorraine, the tornado wheeled over to the jukebox and jostled it so that it started playing "Sweet Home Chicago," a song everyone in the bar detested.

"I'm sorry, Ed," Lorraine said. "I'll sell you packaged goods if you like."

"All right. Give me a six of High Life to go," he said, but he wasn't happy about it. He liked to avoid his apartment walls as much as possible.

Outside, to the tornado, he said, "You're a pain in the ass."

"I'm sorry," the tornado said.

Once safely back in his apartment, with two beers inside him and an old episode of *Fawlty Towers* on TV, Ed finally told the tornado he was ready to talk.

"Can we please turn off the TV?" the tornado said. Manuel was getting beaten about the head by John Cleese.

"As you like," Ed said. "Let's get this over with." He clicked off the TV with the remote.

Now that it finally had Ed's complete attention, the tornado began, "You're probably wondering why I'm here."

"Bingo."

"Well, this isn't easy to explain, but, well, I guess I'm sort of a ghost."

"A ghost tornado?" Ed chuckled. "That's rich."

"What's more," the tornado continued, "I'm your father."

At that Ed choked on his beer.

"Wh-at?"

"That's right, Ed—I'm your dad."

"If you are, you're an asshole," Ed said, narrowing his eyes.

"I may be that, too. That's why I'm here—to ask for your forgiveness."

Ed looked out the window for a moment. His head was full of blood.

"Get the fuck out of here," he said bitterly.

"No Ed, please wait. Listen. When I left your mother, we weren't getting along. I was ruining myself with booze; I wasn't in a good place . . . There was financial difficulty—"

"And your answer to the problem was to leave? That's some solution."

"I—it didn't happen exactly like that. She—your mother told me to get out. She probably didn't tell you that. She wanted me gone. She never wanted to hear from me again. Not even alimony. She wanted me to disappear."

"That's not what she told me," Ed said.

"I know that, Ed, but it's the truth. She wanted to hate me for the rest of her life, and she wanted you to hate me too. I made mistakes, Ed; I'm not saying I didn't. But I left because she asked me to, and that's the truth."

"We didn't know if you were alive or dead," Ed said.

"Well, I'm dead now. A few months ago I got into a traffic altercation in Albuquerque—some guy brained me with a golf club."

"Jesus."

"Ed, I'm here to set the record straight. Things aren't like what you thought. I wanted to be with you. I wanted to help raise you, to come back, but she wouldn't hear of it. She did eventually start to take money, though. I cleaned up, Ed. I got myself straightened out at a rehab place in Oregon. I started a new family—"

"Hold it," Ed said. He didn't want to hear about stepbrothers and sisters. He didn't want to know whether he had them, or anything about them. This was too much information as it was.

"Ed, look, I'm sorry for the way things turned out. I wish you could have had a better upbringing. All I ever wanted was for you to be happy."

"And Mom? What did she want?" Ed asked. "Did she want me to be miserable?"

"It was rough on her, Ed. She was living with a person who was impossible to live with. There was a lot of bile. It wasn't her fault."

"So that's it? I forgive you and then you go away? Back to wherever?"

"That's right, Ed. I won't be a restless spirit anymore—a poltergeist, if you like."

"That's great for you. What do I get out of this?" Ed asked, thinking about how circumstances had reduced him to hawking gym-club memberships in a gorilla outfit.

"You'll close the door on a terrible past. A new door will open; you'll see."

Ed considered.

"All right, Dad, you're forgiven. I forgive you."

"Ed, it doesn't seem like you mean that."

Ed shrugged. "Take it or leave it—you got what you came for. Now get lost."

"Ed, I—"

"Go."

Ed's father moved slowly toward the kitchen, paused a moment, and finally spun through the transom window.

When Ed was sure his father was gone, he rolled up the transom, locked the door, and then returned to the couch and drank off another beer. After some time he picked up the phone and called his mother in Palm Springs.

"Eddie!" she said. "How are you? It's about time you check in with your poor old mother."

"Sorry, Mom. You know how it is—always busy trying to make a buck where I can."

"Speaking of bucks, I won at bingo last night! A thousand dollars!"

"Wow, that's great, Ma. What are you gonna do with the money?"

"Oh, I thought I'd buy this fancy-schmantzy gas grill for the back patio."

"Cool. Hey Ma, um, you haven't, uh, seen Dad recently, have you?"

"Your father? I haven't talked to him a very long time. For all I know, he's dead."

"Yeah." Ed sighed. He suddenly wished he hadn't called.

"You haven't heard from him?"

"No, I was just wondering," Ed said. "So, how's the weather?"

"It dipped down to seventy yesterday, and everyone put their coats on. That's a chilly day down here." She laughed.

"Heh heh. Yeah, that's rough, all right. Say, Ma, this is gonna sound weird, but I've been thinking about Dad a little, and I was just wondering if you, like, still hated him and everything. I mean, if you ever saw him again, would you forgive him?"

Ed's mother paused.

"Ed, it's been a very long time since your dad and I last spoke. You get old enough and the anger fades. It wasn't all his fault, really. You keep hate inside you and you end up with cancer, or something worse."

"What's worse than cancer?"

"Letting go when maybe you should have held on."

Ed looked up at the closed window in the kitchen.

"Hey, Mom, I don't mean to cut this off short, but my landlord is here. He needs to check out a bad pipe in the bathroom."

"OK, well, I'll let you go, then. Give me a call back tomorrow. I'll be home after my computer class at four."

"All right, Mom. Will do."

"I love you, son."

"I love you too."

Ed hung up the phone. He was suddenly very tired, even though it wasn't that late. He went into the kitchen and cranked the transom window wide. He'd sleep better with it open.

Hero

D r. Mayhem captured me as I was going to my car for some smokes. I was almost to the roadside where I'd left the Suburban, looking forward to my first cigarette of the day, when a slight young man with a spotty beard and long ponytail came out from behind a tree and brandished a large blue knife. I recognized him immediately from the photograph I'd seen in the papers, not to mention the poster in the window of the gas station in Beloit.

"Good morning," he said. "Looks like today is your unlucky day."

Generally speaking, of all the possible misfortunes to befall campers in the deep woods—mosquito bites, sunburns, getting lost, meeting with dangerous wildlife—one does not anticipate America's Most Wanted.

Unlucky doesn't really start to cover it.

Among other things, Mayhem was wanted in connection with a series of attempted terrorist acts in Chicago, including poisoning bulldozers, a City Hall blackout, a subway car derailment, an attack on a TV station, and an incident in which the plumbing of Buckingham Fountain had been plugged. Most of these schemes had created only minor inconveniences, but Mayhem was nothing if not a tireless revolutionary.

Just a couple of days before our encounter by the roadside, his twelve-year-old henchman, "Kid Apocalypse," had been found by police holding a bag full of chemicals in a university steam tunnel. Mayhem had narrowly escaped. It was believed that he had fled to the Kettle Moraine forest of Wisconsin.

And they were correct. Here he was.

Mayhem produced a set of handcuffs. "Put these on," he said, "or I'll gut you like a fish faster than you can say 'Babe Winkelman.'"

Forgetting the overt and implied advice of crime prevention pamphlets, cop shows, and serial-killer movies, I did not run. If strangers ever ask you to come with them, statistics show you're better off taking your chances and running like hell while you're free, rather than allowing yourself to get trapped. Whatever happens later will probably be much worse.

"You can take my wallet," I said. "My car—it's right over there. Take it. It's yours."

Mayhem shook his head. "The cuffs," he said. "Put them on. *Now.*" The knife was just inches below my nose, where I could see the edge's white, razor-sharp bevel. I had no doubt that it could slice through the toughest airport luggage material, to say nothing of my paperlike skin.

Not thinking, I put the cuffs on like I was going along with a stupid magic trick. Once I did this, Mayhem relaxed a bit and lowered the knife, and I knew I had committed perhaps the greatest blunder of my life. He attached a piece of nylon cord to the chain between the cuffs and tied the other end to his belt loop.

"Let's go," he said. "March!"

We headed back into the forest, going due north instead of east where my camp and friends were. As we navigated trails that were overgrown with dense foliage, I continued offering my captor whatever I could—my watch, my bank account, my promise to never tell a soul about this.

"No sale," he said. We stopped for a moment before a clearing and looked down on a canopy of trees. Trees as far as the eye could see. Mayhem suddenly took note of my orange baseball hat, which was meant to protect me from hunters. I was surprised it had taken him so long to notice it. He swiped it violently off my head and stuffed it under his flannel shirt.

"So," I said, "am I being held hostage, then?"

"Ding ding. What do we have for him, Johnny?"

"No need to be rude," I said.

"Come on, pick it up. We gotta get to camp."

"You sure you want to do this?" I said. "You could be adding ten to fifteen more years onto your sentence. If you kill me, that's life."

"No, if I kill you, that's *death*," Mayhem said, amused at his own joke. He had an unpleasant tittering laugh, the laugh of a teenage supervillain.

I tried another tack. Reportedly, Mayhem was something of a computer geek, apart from his terrorist tendencies. I tried to appeal to that side of him by offering him my very rare and valuable X-Men comic books, my autographed copy of Kurt Vonnegut's *Timequake*, and a vintage 1968 *Barbarella* movie poster.

"Shut up, Shield," Mayhem said.

"What?"

"That's what you are to me—a shield," Mayhem said. "You're my ticket out of here."

"They're looking for you, Mayhem," I said. "There's no escape. You're best off surrendering as soon as possible."

"What makes you the authority on what I should do?" Mayhem said, raising that knife again. I had to be careful.

"I'm a Spanish teacher?" I said.

This made Mayhem laugh. That was good, I thought. The knife came down. We were walking again.

A half hour later we reached the camp—a secluded recess in a hill with a tall rock overhang. There was a rolled-up sleeping bag; a small fire pit had been dug into the dirt. Just inside the crevice, I could make out a backpack and a laundry bag. He connected me to a chain that was attached to a tree; it allowed me about five meters in any direction.

"So now what?" I asked.

Mayhem was crouched over the fire pit, trying to set an empty bag of Doritos alight with his Bic.

"I need to think," Mayhem said. "The first step was to get a hostage. Now, I plot."

While my captor plotted, a helicopter was suddenly heard in the distance. Its stuttering growl grew louder, causing Mayhem to scramble into the crevice. He returned with a large green tarp and instructed me to cover myself and lie still. After I was hidden by the tarp, Mayhem crouched in his tiny cave.

Once the helicopter was gone, Mayhem uncovered me and started poking at the ashes in the fire pit with a stick.

"You know you can't hide up here forever," I said. "You'll get hungry. You'll get cold. Right now your buddy, that kid they caught in the steam tunnel, is probably telling them everything."

Mayhem stood up and spat.

"Apocalypse betrayed me," he said. "I should have seen that coming. I thought he was going to work out, become a true member of the Freedom Team, but obviously he didn't have the stuff. But just wait. When my next plan is unleashed, the city of Milwaukee will be brought to its knees."

Mayhem's eyes sparked with a kind of insanity I had seen in some of my more unstable students—the ones I'd routinely sent to the dean or the social worker.

"And what plan would that be?" I asked.

Mayhem started pacing the camp, slashing his stick through the air violently.

"What Apocalypse had on him was nothing," Mayhem said. "The *real* stuff is in that cave." He gestured behind me to the laundry sack. "I have enough dynamite in there to blow the bejeezus out of the Mickelschnauzer Brewery."

Instead of asking Mayhem how depriving Milwaukee of one of its breweries was going to have any sort of lasting effect on the infrastructure of capitalism or democracy, I turned to more immediate concerns.

"So how long are we gonna be up here?" I asked. "The FBI is already scouring the forest for you. The best thing to do is get out of here, pronto."

By now I figured my friends Nick and Steve must have reported me missing, and maybe authorities had made the connection that Mayhem could have apprehended me. I hoped dogs were searching the area near my car and had picked up our scent. If we were to walk around, the better the chance that someone would find us.

"No, tonight we stay put," Mayhem said.

I sat down. "In that case, what's for lunch?" I said. "I'm starved." I also wanted a cigarette, but Mayhem, apparently never one of the cool kids, told me he didn't smoke.

Inside the cave, Mayhem had a few cans of Hormel chili and a pot. After watching him mess around with getting a fire started for a half hour I finally begged him to let me do it. Ten minutes later we had a nice fire going and the chili was boiling, ready to eat.

"We'll have to share the spoon, since I only have one," Mayhem said. "I'll eat, then you eat."

As I watched him scarf up the meat chunks, I almost became disembodied, seeing myself from above, noting how quickly life's fortunes can change. One minute, I'd been off on a quiet morning in the woods, looking to kill my nic fit, the next I was chained to a tree, watching the world's most ineffectual anarchist eat chili while the FBI hunted for him.

When it was my turn to eat, Mayhem awkwardly started to ask me questions.

"So, are you married?" he asked.

Remembering that it was good to personalize yourself as much as possible to a would-be killer, I lied and said that I was.

"Mary," I said. "That's her name. We've been married for three years now."

"You married a *Mary*?" Mayhem said.

I nodded.

"Where's your ring?" Mayhem asked.

"Oh, I take it off whenever I'm camping," I said. "I got a kid, too—Joe-Joe. He's six years old."

"Six?" Mayhem said. "You had him before you got married?"

I cursed internally for being such a lousy liar.

"Um, yeah. He was sort of unexpected. We had to wait to get married," I said. "We wanted to do it right, you know? We needed to save up money."

Mayhem seemed to accept that.

"Little Joe-Joe." I said, trying to reinforce the image. "He loves Kool-Aid. He drinks it all day long."

"Sugar's not good for kids," Mayhem said. "It rots their teeth and makes them crazy."

"Yeah, I should watch that," I said. "But it lights up his face whenever you give him a cup of it. He drinks it out of this little Popeye mug he has. It's his favorite."

Would any of this bullshit spare my life? I hoped so.

As night fell, Mayhem and I continued to talk; there wasn't anything else to do. I learned all about how he'd been mentored in high school by a math professor named Kleinschmidt. About how the two of them had had a falling out when Mayhem had revealed his plan to flood the gymnasium. Soon after, Mayhem had dropped out of school. Since then, he'd been engaging in various diabolical schemes and had started work on his manifesto. He'd written about two hundred pages so far, he said. The working title was *Technology and How It Will Destroy Us All*.

"Catchy," I said.

As he explained the manifesto, point by ridiculous point, I had the urge to slap Mayhem and jar loose the stupid ideas in his head. Yes, the world was messed up, I wanted to tell him; deal with it. Causing a few traffic snarls and dousing the mayor in darkness wasn't going to do jack in the long run.

Just before we turned in for the night, we split a bag of peanuts and half a bottle of water. I was dreading the thought of having to sleep exposed on this little cliff all night while wearing handcuffs. There could be bobcats, or other animals, that could have at me. When I mentioned this to Mayhem, he seemed a little bit sorry for me, but not much.

"The revolution's just around the corner," he said. "You'll have to get used to much worse than that before it's all over. Revolution is coming sooner than you think."

With that, Mayhem retired to his cave to go to sleep.

"No, it's not," I said to the cave.

"What?" came his voice back through the darkness.

"I said, 'No, it's not coming.'"

No reply.

I lay flat on my back and tried to get comfortable on my dirt bed. I thought about that bag, supposedly full of dynamite, not thirty meters from me. Was it stable or unstable? I wondered. I thought of Mayhem trekking all around the damp subways of Chicago with his cache of chemicals and explosives. It was incredible that he hadn't blown himself up already.

When morning came, I had a total body soreness that I hadn't experienced in a long time. I felt like I'd spent the night in a boxing ring with a kangaroo. Having gone the first full day in fifteen years without having a cigarette hadn't helped; it felt like ice water was running through my veins.

"Well, I think it's time we flee, Shield," Mayhem said. He was pacing around, snacking on a bit of candy bar.

"Flee?" I asked.

"Yeah, your advice, right? Last night you said we should get out of here."

"Oh yeah. Yes, good idea," I said. I stood and tried to stretch. Walking was going to be very difficult. Every joint in my body was screaming.

"I thought I could wait them out, maybe, but I don't have a lot of food, and I obviously can't go into any stores. We need to get to your car."

I wanted to point out that, from a not-getting-arrested standpoint, this would be about the stupidest move Mayhem could make, since the authorities no doubt had somebody watching my car for this very development, but, of course, I played dumb.

"Yeah, I could drive us someplace. Drive *you* someplace," I clarified, not eager to extend our relationship any more than necessary.

"You think they have your car surrounded?" Mayhem said.

"I don't know. Maybe," I said. "But what other choice do you have?"

"Right. Right," he said. "We should have taken the car right away. Now I see that tactical error."

Just then, from below the ridge, we heard voices and dogs barking. Mayhem's eyes popped wide as he peered over the edge and confirmed his dreaded suspicion.

"They're here," he said.

"Who?"

"The cops and the bloodhounds. They're coming up this way."

"Don't be stupid," I said. "Just surrender. You're young, they'll have some mercy on you."

But Mayhem wasn't listening. "The bastards!" he seethed. "This leaves me only one option."

"What option?" I said, alarmed. "There is no option!"

"Yes, there is," Mayhem said. That evil glint was back in his eye as he crawled into the cave and started rooting around in the laundry bag.

"What was that? What did you do?" I said when he came out a minute later. The bag was still in the cave. The dogs were getting closer.

"You'll see. Just tell the cops I'm hidden in the cave." With that, Mayhem smiled and scrambled off the cliffside facing away from the police. There was a loud commotion of snapping twigs.

"Other side!" I shouted to the cops. "He's on the other side!"

There was a lot of shouting then and a squelched shriek that made me think that maybe Mayhem was no more. Meanwhile, I thought I could hear a crude time bomb behind me, ticking away the seconds.

A bloodhound was the first to peer over the edge. It was barking its head off, and then there were about five guys in blue vests with guns drawn on me. Two others were going toward the cave.

"Don't," I said. "There's a bomb in there."

That stopped them. They seemed unsure what to do, so I spelled it out for them.

"Get me the hell out of these cuffs!" I screamed.

They weren't in time.

—⁓⁓—

We all felt the bomb explode before we saw and heard it. A shock wave hit us, knocking us off our feet. Then there was a short but deafening roar, and a cloud of smoke billowed from the mouth of the cave. The explosion was impressive, but it was nothing on the order Mayhem had probably hoped.

When we all got our bearings and realized that, miraculously, no one had died or sustained more than a ruptured eardrum, I resumed my entreaties to be separated from the tree. As I was guided down from the cliff minutes later, I could see another group of men carrying Mayhem away through the trees ahead of us.

"Is he dead?" I asked.

"Stunned, that's all," a beefy fellow said. "Probably not used to taking the full brunt of a rifle butt to the head. It takes some getting used to."

—⁓⁓—

That day and the next, there was the expected national news bonanza about the capture of the insidious domestic terrorist who called himself Dr. Mayhem. I was treated for minor abrasions by the hospital and given the card of a psychoanalyst, which I figured I probably wouldn't need. I was then reunited with my camping buddies, Nick and Steve, and members of my family, all of whom had feared the worst.

Steve showed me one of the newspaper articles as I was sitting in my hospital bed waiting for my release to be authorized. I was being hailed as a hero by *USA Today*. Outside the hospital, this also seemed to be the prevailing belief among the throng of reporters who swarmed me as I was escorted into a waiting vehicle.

"How does it feel to have saved Milwaukee? Do you feel like a hero?" they asked, jamming microphones into my face.

To be honest, I didn't feel like a hero. I felt pretty much like a regular guy.

"Call me a Spanish teacher who could really use a smoke," I said.

The Painter

The painter was dead in the backyard. Angie came in from taking out the garbage and told me about it as I was cracking eggs into the pan.

"He's dead," she said. "Must have been a heart attack or something."

"Are you sure?" I said. "I mean, did you take his pulse or anything?"

"His pulse? Are you kidding me? I ain't goin' near a dead guy."

"Well, what if he's still alive?" I said.

"Well, go find out for yourself, if you're so interested."

"All right, I will. Watch the eggs," I said. I went outside. It was a nice summer day. I went over to where the old painter was keeled onto his side in his white jumpsuit, a can of paint beside him, and a brush, still wet with white paint, in his hand. He looked dead, all right. I put a couple of fingers under his chin and didn't feel anything.

"Sir? Sir?" I asked, shaking him. He didn't move. I looked around to see whether any of the neighbors were out. I didn't see them. I didn't know what to do, so I took a cigarette from my bathrobe and lit it.

"Is he dead?" Angie called from the window of the kitchen.

I nodded. I stood there. I stood there and smoked. This guy had been hired for the job a couple of days before by my landlord to paint the back garage, and now he was dead. I felt like I should do something but didn't know what. I went back inside. The eggs were ready, and Angie and I sat down and ate them with toast and coffee.

"What do you want to do?" Angie asked.

"I don't know."

"He's dead, you're sure?"

"Yeah, there's no blood moving around inside him."

"That guy, he said hello to me when he arrived," Angie said.

"Yeah."

"I'm the last person he talked to on this earth."

"Yeah."

"That's sorta weird. I didn't even *know* him."

"Yeah."

"He seemed like a nice guy."

"Uh-huh."

"I got a camera," Angie said.

"You got film?"

"Half a roll."

"OK."

Angie got the camera out and I put our plates in the sink. We went outside. I looked for my neighbors again but didn't see any.

"All right, prop him up," Angie said.

"Oh, shit." I lugged the guy up and maneuvered him into a sitting position against the garage.

"Can you get him so his head is up?"

"Jesus."

I worked the guy as best I could. He kept wanting to fall over.

"All right, now make a pose," Angie said.

"Like how?"

"I don't know. Put your arm around him or something."

I crouched down and smiled. Angie snapped one.

"OK, now me."

Angie handed the camera to me and pranced over to the body. She pulled her nightgown up to show some leg. She smiled. I snapped one.

"We could probably get arrested for this," I said.

"Why? We didn't kill him."

"Yeah, I know, but there might be a law we don't know about."

"Since when do you care about laws?"

"Yeah, well, let's get back inside. I've got to call someone."

Angie followed me back in. We poured out some more coffee and had a smoke at the kitchen table. We looked out at the guy. He was still sitting there, and it looked like he was staring at us.

"We should take a picture of just him," Angie said. "It'd make a good album cover."

"Let the dead rest in peace," I said.

"Isn't it a little late for that?"

Just then, the phone rang. It was Duvall from upstairs.

"What's with the guy in the backyard? Is he sick or something?" he asked.

"How should I know?" I said.

"Well, he's scaring my wife," Duvall said.

"What do you want me to do about it?"

"OK," Duvall said. He hung up.

"That was Duvall," I told Angie. "He's worried about the painter." Angie started laughing. She slapped her knee.

"Should we call Salvador?" I asked. Salvador was our landlord.

"I guess we should," Angie said.

I went to the desk and got Salvador's number. I got his machine.

"Salvador, this is Zero," I said, "Y'know that painter you hired to paint the garage? I guess he died. Call me when you get in." I hung up.

"Not home," I told Angie.

"Call the cops," she said.

"That'd be a switch," I said. "Usually someone calls them on *me*."

"That's because you take off your clothes on stage and start fights," Angie said.

"Well, I ain't calling them," I said.

"You better call them. What if one of the Mexican kids next door sees him?"

"They gotta learn about death sometime," I said. But I was picking up the phone. I called 411 by accident. I told them to connect me to 911.

As I waited for the cops to come on, Angie started tickling me.

"911," a woman said.

"Hi, uh, yeah," I said. "A-ha-ha-ha. Cut it out! A-ha-ha-ha-ha!"

"Sir, what's the problem? Can I have your name please?"

"This is Zero," I said.

"Sir, are you in danger? Is there a situation?"

"Um … No, ha-ha-ha … Will you stop it? Ah! Ha-ha-*ha*!" I dropped the phone. Angie hung it up.

"What the hell?" I demanded.

"I was trying to relax you. I know how you get nervous around the cops."

"Shit! What are they going to think?"

The phone rang then. I picked up.

"Hello, this is 911. Did you just phone us?"

"Yeah."

"Is there a problem? We're sending a car over. What's the situation?"

"There's a painter in my backyard," I said.

"That's not a situation."

"I believe he's dead," I said.

"Did someone kill him?" the person said.

"His heart did," I said.

"OK, a car will be over. What is your name?"

"Zero," I said.

"*Full* name, sir."

"Just Zero, that's it." I said.

"OK, Mr. Zero, please wait outside for the squad."

"All right."

I hung up.

"Well, what's happening?" Angie asked.

"They're sending a car over."

I grabbed some jeans, put on a ratty Misfits T-shirt, pulled on my cowboy boots, and went outside to wait. I found Duvall out there by the dead guy, looking at him.

"This guy's dead, looks like," Duvall said.

"Yeah, I just called the cops," I said.

Duvall looked at me funny. I lit a smoke and looked around. The Mexican kids from next door were hanging on the fence, watching us. I saw the cop pull into the gravel alley behind the garage.

Duvall stood up. His wife was shouting something from the window.

"Shut up, ya crazy woman!" he yelled.

A fat cop appeared in front of us.

"Who's Zero?" he said.

"I am."

"What's with the hair? You in a circus?" the cop asked me.

"I'm in a band. Same difference."

"You the guy who called?"

"Yup."

"This the dead guy?"

"Yup."

"Thought so." The cop knelt down and tried for a pulse. Then he stood up and got out a notebook. I heard the back door slam. Angie came across the lawn with a couple of Schlitz beers. She handed one to me.

"Want one?" she asked Duvall.

"Uh, no, thanks," Duvall said. He was trying to follow what was going on.

"When did you find him?" the cop asked me.

"About twenty minutes ago."

"Uh-huh. And do you know the deceased?"

"Just that our landlord hired him to paint the garage and he was doing a pretty poor job of it. Look at all the paint on the plants."

The cop looked at the paint splatters and then turned back to me. "I'm afraid he's not going to be finishing the garage," he said, deadpan.

I guffawed. Angie cracked up. Duvall just looked perplexed.

"All right, where's the landlord?" the cop asked.

"I don't know. I left a message on his machine," I said.

"Give me his name and number. I'm gonna have an ice-cream truck take this guy away."

"Ice cream?" Duvall said.

"I'll get it," Angie said. She ran back inside. I saw the cop watch her go.

"Who're you?" the cop asked Duvall.

"A concerned neighbor."

"Did you see anything? Any suspicious activity?"

"Nope."

"Good enough." the cop said. Just then, he noticed the kids. "Hey you kids!" he shouted, "get your butts inside!"

The kids just smiled and looked at each other. They didn't move.

"Christ on fire," the cop said.

Duvall went to his porch and returned with a potato sack. He covered the body with it. Angie gave the cop Salvador's number.

The cop went to the squad to call for an ambulance. Mrs. Duvall shouted something from the window again.

"I'm coming, you crazy woman!" Duvall shouted back. He walked over to the kids and gave them a couple of dollars.

"Get outta here," he said. "Go rot your teeth out someplace."

The kids scattered.

Angie and I sipped our beers, and Duvall went inside. Pretty soon the ambulance showed up. They hauled the painter away and that was that. The cop took off, and we were all back to our lives. Angie picked up the paintbrush and laid a couple of strokes onto the wood. The garage wasn't even half-done.

"What a sad way to die," Angie said.

"Yeah."

We went back to the apartment, got high, and turned on the Saturday morning cartoons, which were still going.

We watched Wile E. Coyote fall off a cliff and come back to life.

Stormbringer

One morning, Isaac awoke from uneasy dreams to find himself transformed into a Norse warrior. He looked in wonder at his hand, which had just smashed his alarm clock to bits. It was raw and red and was twice its normal size, at least. The inner palm was calloused to a hard leather, as if he worked as a rancher rather than as a money lender.

"By Odin's Gate!" he cried. His voice was a thunderous roar that made the ceiling bulb shake. Some plaster fell.

"Isaac, get up now," his mother called from the other side of the bedroom door. "You don't want to be late for work."

Isaac clasped his hands to his mouth and, to his astonishment, found he had grown a long white beard overnight.

"By the saints of Valhalla!" he whispered. Ripping off his bed sheets, he examined his body. It was rigid and muscular, scarred and veined. His privates were wrapped in a fur pelt of some sort, and large iron bracelets ringed his ham-sized wrists.

"Isaac!" his mother called again. "Your coffee's ready! Hurry up now!"

"Be still, woman!" Isaac roared, knocking down more plaster and setting off a car alarm in the street.

"Isaac! What's gotten into you?" his mother asked, her voice quavering with concern. Her footfalls stopped outside his door.

Isaac quickly stuck out a foot and clamped it against the door. His mother pushed uselessly against it.

"Isaac? Isaac!" she called, hammering her palm against the door. "Is something wrong? Open up! Are you sick?"

Holding the door secure with one hand, Isaac dragged a chest of drawers over to keep it in place.

"Sick," he said.

"But Isaac, you can't miss work. You've never missed work," his mother said in a panicky voice. Isaac sighed and sat back on his bed, which creaked noisily beneath him. He drew a small mirror from his desk drawer and examined his face.

His skin looked weathered beyond time. His face was cragged and ruddy, like a homeless person's. His eyes, normally mud brown, were blue and smoky. His hair ran down to his shoulders.

As he sat contemplating what to do, he began to smell wondrous scents. Breakfast, cooking on the stove. He thought of his usual bland bowl of Toastie-Os and how such fare would hardly make a dent. His mother was obviously making a nice breakfast in hopes of luring him out of the room.

Presently, there was another knock on the door. This time it was his stepfather, Brian.

"Come on, Isaac!" he called. "You can't be so sick that you can't put in a few measly hours pushing paper around."

When was the last time Brian had put in a few hours of work doing anything? Ever since getting laid off from his groundskeeping job six months before, all he'd seemed good for was keeping his mother company on the couch watching daytime TV, drinking Bud Light, and smoking discount cigarettes.

A sudden rage filled Isaac. He threw the dresser aside and ripped the door open, burying the handle in the wall in the process. Brian stood goggle-eyed, dressed in his usual garb—a loose-fitting Chicago Bears sweatshirt and gray sweatpants. Just beyond him, Isaac's mother almost dropped the frying pan.

"*Wh-at?*" Isaac bellowed at the stick-like Brian, almost blowing him down. His stepfather scuttled behind his mother, who stood transfixed. Isaac sniffed powerfully and motioned toward the steaming eggs.

"Well, woman," he said. "Let's have the grub!"

His mother tilted the eggs onto a plate. "Isaac, is that you?" she burbled. "Is this my Isaac?"

Ignoring her, Isaac took the plate, opened his mouth, and shoveled it all down in three great handfuls.

"Is that all you have?" he roared. "It nary gave me but a taste!"

"It's those pills," Brian sputtered from the corner. "He's taking ephedra, I bet."

With a swift and powerful thrust, Isaac reached out and throttled Brian by the neck, shaking him violently like a puppet. Brian's knees snapped back and forth, and a pack of cigarettes fell out of the waistband of his sweats.

"Stop it! Stop it!" Isaac's mother screeched. She swatted at Isaac's arm with her spatula.

Isaac put Brian back down but continued to grin at him.

"Shut your mouth, chicken man," he said.

Rubbing his throat, Brian started towards the living room, grumbling under his breath. "Damn kid gonna make me miss *Maury*."

Isaac's mother popped four slices of bread into the toaster, began cracking more eggs into the pan, and added in some bacon strips.

"Maybe you'll feel better after you're all filled up," she said. "Maybe you'll be able to make it in to work today after all."

"Bah!" Isaac said. He stomped to the back porch, just outside the kitchen, and regarded the traffic congealing on Chicago Avenue with disdain. He stuck out a gnarled hand, palm towards the sky.

"By the power of Aegir!" he called out.

Moments later, the sky darkened as clouds smashed together. The August sun was vanquished; lightning would now be responsible for all of the sky's light. It flashed in terrible harsh streaks and made ear-shattering whip cracks. A bolt hit a nearby traffic light and sent it blinking out of commission. Torrents of rain hurtled down, making a quick shallow river of the streets.

Isaac returned to the kitchen with a wide smile on his face.

"Work has been called off due to rain delay," he said.

His mother left the stove to inspect the fierce weather and the ensuing chaos. People were running for cover from the blowing winds and rain. While she was absorbed by the purple sky and the lightning show, Isaac greedily scraped the hot food into his mouth.

He returned to his room, lay back on his puny bed, and closed his eyes. In minutes he was asleep, and he was soon dreaming about mighty clashes with murderous adversaries and romance with enchanting maidens.

At various intervals, Isaac would awaken and catch bits of conversation—his hearing, it seemed, had become super-acute.

"He isn't feeling well today. Yes, we appreciate that but really, he's sick and—really, you shouldn't—"

Sometime later, Isaac returned to full consciousness. The front door had been opened. There was a visitor. Distinctly, he made out the voice of his employer, Mr. Reynolds.

"No, no. It's no trouble at all," he said. "Let me take these galoshes off. This weather's really something, eh? A cup of coffee? Well, sure, that would be great."

Isaac heard his mother move to the kitchen, saying "Oh, he's quite sick, I'm afraid. He's resting now. He's really not at all himself today."

The TV in the living room resounded with jeers and laughs. Some other abominable talk show was on. The audience brayed like donkeys.

"Really, you shouldn't have come," she said.

"Well, I know this is unusual. I wouldn't have come by but for the fact that we're having a major computer problem this morning and Isaac always seems to know what to do in these cases. I thought I might be able to convince him to come in for just a bit to fix the glitch."

Isaac's mother returned to the living room and gave Mr. Reynolds the coffee.

"So, what kind of fever does he have?" he asked.

Brian and Isaac's mother looked at each other.

"Oh, he's been pukin'," Brian said matter-of-factly. "He's pukin' sick."

"That's certainly a shame," Mr. Reynolds said. He sipped at the bitter coffee and let his eyes rest on Springer's guests—Rich Girls Who Marry Hillbilly Trash. "Poor guy. Do you think I could talk to him?"

Once again, Brian and Isaac's mother's eyes locked.

"Don't want to catch what he's got," Brian said. "He's pukin' sick, like I said. In fact, I think it's time I check the bucket for him."

Brian stood up abruptly. Isaac's mother's eyes burned like laser beams into his back.

"Hey, maybe I'll come with," Mr. Reynolds said, darting up to follow, but neither went far. Isaac was standing in the dining room blocking them.

Mr. Reynolds turned white-green and his mouth fell open like a drawbridge. Isaac was gnawing on a piece of cold turkey leg.

"Mr. Reynolds," he spat, "what brings you here? And in such inclement weather as this?"

Mr. Reynolds rattled, "I—Isaac? Is that you under all that makeup? Why, is it a costume holiday of some sort? Or is this some kind of prank you're pulling?"

In reply, Isaac knocked the bulbous, toylike head of his employer clean off and sent it tumbling to rest in front of Brian's feet.

"Uh—ugh!" Brian managed, leaping away from the head.

Isaac rested a large hand on his mother's weary shoulder.

"You shan't be bothered again by this unwelcome vermin," he assured her. "Now, dearest mother, it strains my heart to tell you this, but your restless son must again voyage—the land of Bifröst calls!"

And with that, Isaac swaggered through the door, leaving the warm corpse of Mr. Reynolds for them to deal with.

Outside, it was still a torrential downpour. Isaac scoured the streets for maidens, but found none. On a nearby street with clogged storm drains, several motorists were trying to push their vehicles out of knee-deep water.

This was not maiden weather, Isaac decided. Once again he appealed to Aegir, and presently the rains ceased and a huge, fiery sun appeared. Isaac started towards the premier swank coffee shop in his neighborhood, a clean, well-lighted place called Letizia's.

Inside the warm, glowing confines of the shop, about twenty people stood cowering around their java mugs, peering anxiously at the recently venomous skies. Several faces recoiled when Isaac blotted out the newly revealed sunlight. He entered the shop and eyed the speechless crowd. He spied several fine lasses that would do just fine.

"Aye," he said in a cracked and terrible voice. "I'm looking for a fair maiden or two to join me on a wondrous sea voyage across the Aegean, into the Mediterranean, and beyond!"

The only person moving in the shop was the tiny barista, who ignored the ogre and continued making cappuccinos.

Isaac's eyes rested upon a pretty, pale, but enticing blonde.

"I say, you of the fair skin and voluptuous amounts, what of my offer? One cannot travel in a more fine manner than with the Stormbringer! What say you?"

The girl's mouth opened like a sock drawer in an earthquake, but nothing came out. A collective sigh of relief went through the room; with the freakish monster's attention so focused on the girl, perhaps they could make it out alive.

"Eh, woman? Speak up! I cannot hear you."

"I, uh, I have errands to run today," the woman said meekly.

Little fires danced in Isaac's eyes.

"Bah! What is more exciting than a tour with the Legion of Torpor? Will you see the captive monster of Golemdale today? Will you feast at Corpsmort? Will you bask in the splendor of Swineville?"

"Really," the woman said. "I have laundry to do."

"Argh! You're not fit to accompany a cat to a saucer, much less to sail with a mighty warrior! If it is not smog you breathe, it is the scent of your own decomposition!"

The woman looked affronted, but she also seemed glad that the behemoth's interest in her seemed to be waning. In a corner, a man in vintage eyewear scribbled Isaac's speech into his writing journal. He could probably get it published as a free-verse poem in *Hollow Concept*.

"Any takers? Who has the will and courage to leave this city of devils? I could always use a good oarsman or two." Isaac's eyes shifted between the men in the shop.

"Alas, it looks like ye could hardly hoist a piglet, much less compel a sailing craft across the ocean," Isaac said, exasperated. "Oh, to Niflheim with you!" He crashed back outside.

By now, people were slowly venturing onto the streets again, most of them looking cautiously at the sky. Isaac stomped down Division Avenue, using the street as his sidewalk. Cars honked and swerved around him. On his journey east, he stopped only once: at a gas station, where he gobbled down a dozen Zagnut bars and a gallon of milk.

When at last he reached the lake, he walked down a concrete pier and stood beside a Latino fisherman. He looked into the distance.

"Is this what passes for water in these parts?" he asked the man.

"*Ai, si*," the man said.

"'Tis but a trickle," Isaac said. "I have seen more current in a glass of ale!"

The man nodded uncertainly. His young son was bouncing up and down and pointing to Isaac. "*Esta Hulka! Esta Hulka!*"

Isaac lifted the boy in the air, much to the child's screaming delight, and gently placed him back down.

"Eat your venison," Isaac told him, "and you will grow up to be 'Hulka' too."

With that message imparted, Isaac ventured back to the mainland and inspected a hot dog stand with a giant fiberglass wiener on top of the roof. In seconds, Isaac had the object in his hands and was carrying it away, ignoring the bewildered protests of the vendor.

"This will do until I find a crew to join up with," Isaac said, plucking a green slat out of a park bench to use as an oar. After ensuring that his boat was waterproof, Isaac pushed out into the greenish waters and implored Aegir for a strong wind to blow at his back.

Isaac was not sure where he should go, so he just rowed directly out until, in the distance, there appeared a mighty vessel. It was huge and white, with blinking lights and impressive stature. Isaac pointed his meager craft toward it. Who knew what mission it was on—perhaps treasure hunting or sea-serpent slaying, or maybe it was just the US Navy on maneuvers. Whatever it was, Isaac tingled inside, thinking of the adventure that awaited him.

All This And More

By the time she was fifteen, my adopted daughter Lily reassumed her given name, Lien, outsourced my parenting skills to Vietnam, and had plans for running a pharmaceutical supply company out of the garage. My wife, Tara, who still held the mantle of mother to Lien, and who had encouraged early initiatives like violin lessons, computer skills, and ballet, now worried, as I did, that Lien's recent interest in stock trading and cryptography was unusual for a teenage girl—one who should have been gabbing on the phone for hours and replacing one hunk with another on her bulletin board rather than doing complex puzzles and studying commodities futures. When Lien asked Tara if she could use the other side of our two-car garage, a.k.a. *my* side, to store medical products for her new Internet start-up, my wife came to me.

I was in my study, working on a novel tentatively titled *The Gutta-Percha Disaster*. Fifteen months had been invested so far. It wasn't going well.

"I don't know what to tell her," Tara said. "If I say no, she always has ten good reasons why I should say yes."

One of the reasons, in this case, was that my car had a vapor-locking problem and had sat idle for the past four months. Lien would doubtlessly argue that her online business would create significant capital that could be used to pay rent for the space, while my broken car wasn't doing anything for anybody. And she would be right.

I scratched my author's beard and tapped a no. 2 pencil on my desk—the same desk on which I had written my one and only best-seller, *Frederico's Leap,* and said, "Why don't you ask Quan?"

Quan was everything I was not. Quan was not an also-ran author with no employable skills. Quan was not a bust-out as a provider to his family. No, what Quan was was a humble, sun-soaked Vietnamese fisherman whose efforts in Nha Trang fed and clothed nine family members. He was also Lien's "Online Father" who dispensed advice in neat, Zen-like increments, like candy tossed across the sea.

"Quan will say I should let her," Tara said. "He'll say, 'Don't stand in the way of a tree,' or something."

"Quan knows best," I said. "Hell, I'll move the car right now."

"No, wait. Do it tomorrow. Let her worry for one night that I won't let her."

"Fine."

———

The next day, as I was pushing my compact out of the garage, a green-and-blue truck arrived, and a mail-delivery person emerged with boxes. Lien popped out the back door in her Hello Kitty T-shirt, looked at me with her dark, inscrutable eyes, and signed for the shipment.

The way it was with us, I didn't need to read Lien's eyes to know what she thought of me. Ever since I'd denied her plea to join NASA's Early Astronauts program two years before, we'd been at a stubborn impasse—for her part, marked by infrequent communication and stealth; for my part, refusing to let a teenage genius run all over me.

I longed for the days when we used to take long bike rides in the park and make monthly trips to the zoo. Our wonderful expeditions to the local library. The days when I still had something to teach her.

Did I regret not letting her join Early Astronauts? No, I did not. That program would have come with a bill of twenty thousand dollars, and I didn't see how preparing Lien for outer space was going to help our struggling family unit. I had made a little bit of money from my big novel, but not so much that I could drop twenty Gs so my daughter could dance in zero gravity.

Lien started unpacking her newly arrived items onto an old metal shelf. Her hackles rose as I came into the garage to inspect what was going on. I saw open boxes full of vaginal cream and jock-itch powder.

"What's cookin', Chief?" I said. "Or maybe I should say, 'What's scratchin', Jackson?'"

Lien hated it when I used colloquialisms, and I had many; I had more sayings than Picasso had paint. She removed a box from my hand and put it back on the shelf.

"Embarrassing products," Lien said. "They sell well on the Internet."

I paused, recalling a purchase of hemorrhoid cream at my local grocery store—a purchase that had caused the line behind me to grind to an agonizing halt while someone ran to do a price check. Maybe Lien was onto something.

"What's the name of your company?" I asked.

"Embarrassing Products," Lien said.

"Just make sure we don't get sued," I said. "Something goes wrong, it's my ass."

Lien kept stocking.

"I have a product for that," she said.

That evening at dinner, I reported the details of our daughter's new business to my wife.

"Yeah, I know," Tara said. "It's actually a good idea, I think. I bet there are a lot of people who'd rather not purchase adult diapers with their cornflakes in public."

Although Lien was busy with her new venture, she still found time to attend classes at Falloncrest High, where she excelled in everything from music to physics. Parents and teachers would sometimes corner us and compliment her. "You must be so proud of your daughter," they'd say. Or, "You two are so lucky."

Tara and I could only smile, pained. Yes, Lien was gifted—champion of the chess club, stellar student, accomplished violinist, promising cryptographer, and budding entrepreneur—but did anyone ever consider the benefits of *nonaccomplishment*? Of sitting tranquilly as the world, and all of its memberships, awards, and clubs, slid by?

Quan, her Online Father, had.

In an ongoing electronic dialogue, Quan advised Lien to incorporate some non-striving and meditation into her life to restore balance. In Quan's words: "A person of great wisdom is like water, which, though benefiting all things, never strives." Thus, I was not surprised when I eventually received a request for permission to erect a polyurethane modular meditation chamber in our backyard.

"I already have the one I want picked out," Lien said. "A company in Tampa sells them. I have the money to pay for it."

As usual, there was no argument Lien could not defeat. She could have gone toe to toe with Mike Wallace in a *60 Minutes* interview.

"What can I say, Madame Secretary?" I replied. "I would be a fool to tell you not to follow a fisherman's advice."

And so the modular shack was shipped from Florida. It looked like the kind of thing you'd find at a security checkpoint for the Center for Disease Control. It was red and white and boxy, and sort of futuristic, like a space pod. Lien put it on the east side of the maple tree in the backyard and hung drapes on the windows so she could meditate unobserved.

I could see the pod from my study, and I will admit to having felt a pang of jealousy at her new digs. As a writer, I needed my private space, too. Why hadn't I ever considered such a thing for myself?

The novels I could write in a thing like that, I thought, snapping my pencils in fury.

As Embarrassing Products' success grew, so did Lien's inventory. Before long, her stock was encroaching on Tara's side of the garage.

One day, we noticed a girl with hair the colors of a multi-flavored snow cone preparing shipments. When asked her name, the girl replied, "Natalie." When this didn't match up to the name Lien provided later that night, Lien stabbed her Caesar salad and said, "Who cares *what* her name is? To me her name is *Cheap Labor*."

Someone from the local newspaper called. They wanted to do a story on Lien and her business. Unaware that he was merely a pawn in a twelve-point buzz-marketing plan, the hapless reporter who arrived for the interview was taken to Lien's room, to the garage, and into her meditation chamber. He was even introduced to Quan, who had this to say: "No form, no sound. Here I am: snow-white peaks, river cutting through the valley."

By the time he was through processing Quan and cataloging Lien's list of storied accomplishments, the poor slob didn't know where to start. The story, published a week later, reflected his disorganization and lack of focus. It wasn't his fault; no one knew how to get a bead on Lien. There were not enough hours in a day to do everything she did.

The interesting thing about the piece was that it told Tara and me several things about Lien that we didn't know. For instance, we didn't know that Harvard was offering her a scholarship, or that InfoDyne Industries was courting her for post-college employment. We didn't know that Lien was cyberdating a semipro downhill skier from Scandinavia, or that she was corresponding with an eighty-five-year-old jailed nuclear activist.

Tara and I were hardly referred to except for the mention that we were artists. Tara was a "watercolorist," and I was an author of fiction thrillers, such as *Everything On It* and *The Snapdragon Conspiracy*, who "hasn't had anything out in years."

Time passed like a trailer in a tornado. Without help from us, Lien learned how to drive and used the money from her booming business to buy a Corvette. Soon after, she sold Embarrassing Products to a competitor for an estimated $1.2 million and began development on other, now-well-established innovative businesses and products: Fear No Bagels, EarthDrink, WhipCrack Gum, and You've Got Pants.

Where did Lien get her ideas? "The MedPod," she told *Business Week* and *Forbes*. "I owe my clarity of vision to my Online Father's suggestion to meditate each day for one hour, minimum."

Meanwhile, Tara continued to paint, and occasionally sell, her wonderful watercolor landscapes, and I continued to struggle with my unfinished novel.

On the eve of Lien's graduation from high school, I prepared a gourmet dinner with fish caught by Quan and shipped via Lien's latest business: Flying Fish, a rapid fish-delivery service that enabled fresh seafood to reach restaurants in the remotest land-locked locations, such as Kansas, within hours. Quan attended dinner via remote link-up, eating from his wooden bowl in Vietnam. At the conclusion of dinner, Lien mentioned she had some big news. Tara and I braced ourselves. This was it. What would become of our bright young daughter? Quan's eyes grew large as he smiled in anticipation, perhaps hoping the surprise would be ice cream for dessert.

"I'm going to Harvard in the fall," Lien said, ending the suspense, "and then, after college graduation, I'm going to join the space program. NASA has already accepted my pre-application."

For the briefest of seconds, Lien's eyes caught mine, and I could read the message written on every dart they shot at me in indelible, poison ink: *You cannot stop me. I will succeed.*

I nodded and sipped my Chianti as I looked at Quan, who was grinning and clapping enthusiastically.

"Well, what do you think of *that*, Quan?" I said. "You can't beat that with a stick, can ya?"

Through his computer translator, Quan cautiously agreed: "White clouds gather east and west. Do you know where the path lies? The path leads from sky to sky."

As Lien moved effortlessly through her college years, spawning successful products and thriving industries, Tara and I heard less and less *from* her and more and more *about* her. We began experiencing our daughter solely as a media event. You couldn't pick up a magazine in a dental office or pluck one from the back of an airplane seat without Lien staring at you in glossy high-def, discussing her flourishing capitalistic empires or speaking optimistically of her lifelong goal to be an astronaut. Now the official spokesperson for MedPod, she would also sometimes enter our home via late-night TV, promising results in four to six weeks.

Lien's entry to the space program was much heralded by media outlets worldwide. Enter any cheeky space phraseology you can think of; the papers and newsmagazines went headline-wild with it. For instance: "Young Entrepreneur Trades Bagels for Stars." Google reconfigured their letters in pictorial honor to her on their homepage for a day. David Letterman even had her on as a guest.

By the time of her inaugural space mission, Tara and I calculated that we had not heard from Lien in over two years. Still, we tried to wish her luck with a bon-voyage wreath sent to her public relations department in Vancouver. Who knows if they bothered to deliver it.

Like almost everyone else, Tara and I watched the blastoff on our TV set. Inside the rocket was a full complement of genius men and women—certainly some of the best and brightest this world had recently produced. They were going into orbit to staff a space station and run various tests. Their mission would keep them in space for the better part of one year.

When the image of the rocket arching into the sky suddenly bloomed into a flower of orange and white flame, I felt a crushing blow to my stomach like a horse had kicked me. As the commentator began to wail in horror, I started to cry. All the ice and distance between Lien and me melted instantly. Tara's fingers extended toward the TV as bright spots of ember fountained downward through the Florida sky like the flower we had named our daughter after.

"*Lily* . . ." she sobbed.

That night we went into Lily's abandoned MedPod, which I had turned into my writing space. Novel drafts lay scattered in piles on the floor. They may as well have been dust.

We contacted Quan and found him grieving, eyes red-rimmed. We told stories of Lily to each other.

Tara and I recalled the tiny, shy girl who had arrived on our doorstep twenty-one years before, holding hands with a caseworker. She had worn a plaid skirt, white stockings, and shiny black little-girl shoes. Tara and I had fallen over each other asking what we could get her, how we could make her happy and comfortable.

For the longest time, Lily hadn't responded, but finally, after being offered every food and drink item in the house, she'd returned to the one she'd wanted all along.

"Popsicle," she'd said.

Tara had fled to the kitchen freezer like there was a fire to put out and offered her five flavor choices. She'd chosen banana.

Quan nodded and said: "While the flower withers, late-spring warblers sing their hearts out. A village of drifting petals."

It was unclear if he knew what a popsicle was, and, I suppose, it didn't matter. What mattered was that Lily would not be forgotten—not by us, not by Quan. What mattered was that we grieved as one, under the stars, as a family.

To Tell About It

I n this world, I am a reporter writing a book about the near-death experiences of others. There is no religious agenda here; I just want the facts. I want to know how you almost died. I am doing this book for selfish reasons. Mainly, because I think it's a good idea for a book, but also because I once had a near-death experience of my own. Stupidly, I almost died when I was seventeen. I attempted to swim across the Illinois River, a body of water that claims at least ten lives every year.

On that foolish night, I miscalculated distance and overestimated my strength. Halfway across the black river, I saw that the shore I'd believed to be on the other side was actually a vertical bank of concrete. I wouldn't be able to rest on the other side for the return trip. Realizing this, I panicked and started back the way I'd come. Soon, I was exhausted. My arms felt weighted down by sandbags. I was taking water down my throat, gasping, barely keeping my head above the river.

I recalled that doing a back float could help in a situation like this and, as I extended my arms and looked up at the sky, I prayed that I wouldn't die. I kicked and floated, kicked and floated, encouraged by my friends, who were watching this spectacle in horror. I made progress slowly, the cold water licking at my ears, occasionally flashing over my eyes. Inch by agonizing inch, I closed the gap to safety.

When at last I was on shore, shivering, my lungs burning, I turned to see a heavy, silent barge float right down the center of the river where I'd been not seconds before.

This was death I witnessed, ominous and lethal as a shark.

For my stupidity, I was awarded an indelible lesson: in seconds your life, any life, can be snuffed out without ceremony, without negotiation. This is what I'm going to write about.

I put out ads. I talk to people. I talk to people who know people. I meet for coffee, for dinner, over beers. I bring my voice recorder. I ask people how they almost died, and they tell me.

A woman tells me how she almost died whitewater rafting on a Class IV river in Wisconsin. A guide who should have known better took this woman and her inexperienced friends down rapids meant for seasoned rafters. Everyone in the boat, including the guide, flew out as they went over a large fall. They were all flung into the churning, uncompromising water.

This woman found herself below the raft, drowning, her head touching the rubber bottom. Her hands sought the edge, but couldn't find it. She needed air. She was pushed down and aside, pulled by current and slammed into rock. The raft moved on and she rode the rapids the rest of the way, swallowing water, bashing her limbs, cracking her helmet, until a tow line was finally thrown to her fifteen minutes later when she was into calmer water. This woman relives her near-death as she tells me the story. She will not raft again; sounds of rushing water terrify her to this day.

A man named Peter tells me about an odd incident that took place while he was driving his car to his girlfriend's place to pick her up for a Neil Young concert. This was years ago, around the time of the first Gulf War, Desert Storm. Peter saw strange flashes of light in the sky— blue-white and brilliant—just ahead. This was odd, since there was no humidity; no storm had been predicted.

"I thought maybe we were under attack by Saddam," he says.

He drove toward the light. The flashing continued. It got brighter. Suddenly he was stopped. The traffic halted. A car directly in front of him backed into his car, a small bumper collision. It was then he saw the giant power cable lying on the street in front of a bus just ahead. The end of the cable was sputtering sparks, twisting like an angry snake. The ground throbbed and hummed. The bus was on fire. People were screaming, shouting for help. Some were running down the street.

"You could smell the current," Peter says. "It was like this live, pissed-off beast."

A man died trying to escape the burning bus. The next morning the story was on the front page of the *Tribune*.

"That bus was just one car-length ahead of me," Peter says, shaking his head. "If I'd left just thirty seconds earlier, the power line would have been on top of my crappy little Toyota. It would have been *me*."

I am told about a subway derailment and fire in the tunnel below the Chicago River. A man describes the course of events:

"First there's a noise, a guttural bang and a weird groan, like a wrench opening a rusty pipe. This is followed by eerie silence. The lights of the El car flicker and die. There's no communication over the intercom from the train conductor. Nothing. At this point I and every one of the six hundred other passengers on this train are thinking the same thing—*terrorist attack*. This is only six months after 9/11. Terrorism is on everyone's mind. I'm wondering if a bomb went off and we're going to see the tunnel and car become flooded. What if the river breached the barrier? I'm thinking this when suddenly, the train car fills up with smoke. It's a vile white smoke, acrid stuff, just horrible. It's got a metal smell to it. It burns your eyes. At that point everyone stands up at once and the emergency door release is pulled. We herd onto the catwalk, into the thicker smoke. People are screaming '*Hurry up! Hurry up! There's fire back here!*' but you can't go any faster because the walkway is only a foot wide and there's people in front of you. We walk through the black tunnel, using our shirt fronts as filters to breathe through. Some people try to light the way with their cellphones. This whole time, I'm thinking I might die. Only when I see the actual exit, a metal ladder headed up to the street—until I see the hatch opening up to the sky, a fireman coming down—do I realize I'm gonna live. When I get up to street level and see my shirt, it looks like I smoked a pack of cigarettes through it."

I do this for months, gathering stories for the collection. I hear stories of a robbery at gun point, of a man stabbed by a homeless drug addict outside a gas station, of a deer that nearly decapitated a mother of two.

I hear from a man who was traveling in India for a software company, whose morning habit for the week he was there was to get a coffee and bagel at a German bakery near his hotel in Mumbai. One morning, he skipped the bagel and coffee—the morning terrorists blew up the bakery.

I hear from a woman who was gardening in her backyard. She was called away by her phone, which was ringing in the kitchen. A minute later a transformer blew, right near where she was standing, and set her fence on fire.

There are other stories: a vicious dog attack on a jogger in a Cook County forest preserve, a man who fell from a tree helping his friend prune some limbs, a lung-cancer survivor, a brain trauma from a hockey puck, a motorist who survived a head-on collision, pneumonia, heatstroke, hypothermia, the gamut.

My life is active with these near-deaths. For nearly a year I'm constantly on the go, running from place to place, always anxious to hear the next story. At one point I have enough stories, but they keep coming in. I can't say no. *One more*, I tell myself, *just one more . . .*

Story One Hundred is from a female comedian. I meet her at her favorite bar—a place where lots of actors come. This woman is short with dark hair, very attractive. She has an unbelievable story about how, one night three years ago, she was drinking and watching the fireworks with friends from atop a condemned parking garage in the city. When the show was over, instead of taking the stairs back down, she went into an elevator shaft, thinking there was a car there, but there wasn't. She fell three stories. Her injuries were severe and life-threatening. She was in the hospital for months recovering.

I have to stop her here, because I know this story.

"But wait," I say, "didn't you die?"

This makes her laugh. "Apparently not," she says, rubbing her arms. She shows me the article in the paper, an article I wrote. It looks the same as I recall, except for the ending. It doesn't fit. I'm certain this woman died. But how can I say that without being rude?

"You look like you don't believe that I'm alive," she says.

"I just don't remember it this way," I say. "Of course I'm glad you survived."

"Well, isn't living just being *pre-dead* anyway?" she asks.

One of her stand-up jokes, I guess.

I wake up laughing with tubes in my arms, a monitor bleeping. I am surrounded by a doctor and nurse and, later, by older versions of my family and friends. The news comes to me gently that I've been in a coma for three years. I was shot in the back while responding to a noise complaint on the West Side.

It comes back to me who I am. I'm not a reporter. I'm a police officer. I'm not writing a book.

I can't speak yet, but I can communicate with a keypad device. I ask about the comedian. She was so real, so vivid. It seems like she's still around me, hovering. I can smell her perfume.

No one knows anything about a comedian.

"You're disoriented," the doctor says. "That's to be expected."

The story comes out the next day, July 5th, in the newspaper I so desperately crave. A young talented female comedian was killed when she fell down an elevator shaft in a parking garage the night before—the night I woke. There is a photo. This is the woman I met in the bar.

I look for the name of the reporter who wrote the story. His name is Phil Rodgers. I may know little about current events, but I know that this man has a file cabinet full of notes, a voice recorder full of voices.

I tell the nurse that I need to contact this man urgently.

I need to tell him how close to death I really came.

And You

*H*ouse Beautiful magazines are stacked in a neat, unread pile. Scents abound—sandalwood, berry blossom, potpourri—assaulting the air, driving me to windows. The furniture is colonial, dusted, polished, expensive, uncomfortable. My aunt is thin, poised, translucent, scented, arid. Sometimes, we go to church bazaars. My days are cleaning, gardening, and soaps. My nights are reading Judy Blume books and my old Strawberry Shortcake lockable diary. Eight weeks ago, my days (and nights) were needles.

I wonder if Pat Sajak thinks about suicide. I wonder if entertainment is the number one American export. I wonder if having babies is worth it.

There's this sign near this church I have to go to on Sundays. It pretends to be the voice of God. Every day there is a new saying from God on the board.

God says: Hi.

God says: I saw that.

God says: Smile, I love you.

I want to have God say something else.

God says: I don't care about you.

God says: Just try me.

God says: I don't need your approval.

God says: You're on your own.

God says: I created this mess.

God says: Use Jesus Motor Fuel—Put a savior in your tank!

My brain is moving in fits and starts. These Blume books are helping.

Whenever I see the neighbor's dog, this dopey Irish setter, I find myself becoming jealous—jealous of a dog. The dog has never smoked a cigarette; it has never gone down on somebody for money. It has never done heroin.

I wanna be your dog. — Iggy Pop

The only men in this town during the day are service men. Men with mail. Men with tools, mowers, and cars. Men standing on grass with giant hoses, spraying chemicals onto lawns. There are tanned, bored, radioactive housewives everywhere, directing them.

The high school kids are from another planet. Planet Wholesome Good Time. Planet Milk in the Cookie Constellation. The kids are white, smart, and strong. The kids are going places. The kids are really saying "no" here.

Sometimes I am sad about the most ridiculous things. I could be sad about my wasted youth or something, but instead I find myself feeling sad about the left-out drummers—Pete Best (the Beatles), Chad Channing (Nirvana), John Rutsey (Rush)—all kicked out before fame hit. This is sadness to me.

My aunt tells me to wash off that apple before I eat it. Chemicals, she says. I want to tell her my body will laugh at any chemical sprayed on an apple.

The library in town is interesting. When I go in to get a library card, they ask me what district I'm in. Like I have any idea.

"Where do you live?" one of them says.

Another one says, "We're gonna need some ID."

In this town, even the librarians talk like cops.

I spend time in the library. It's better than in the antiseptic house. The time away worries my aunt. Sometimes I think she has a librarian spy looking after me. I have fun trying to figure out which one it is.

There are paintings you can "check out" here. They're placed along the walls near the book stacks. Most are pictures of sailboats, gardens, children with flowers, winterscapes, barns, lakes, and fishermen. There is not a single abstract painting here. Apparently no one here feels abstract.

Sometimes I eat lunch by the train tracks, the tracks that go north and south. The tracks that took me here from the city. Sometimes I watch people board, heading that way. I imagine getting on, meeting up with Ellie, cranking in an alley someplace. It's not something I'm likely to do, but I still think about it, how opposite it is. The other day I saw a deer in the train station parking lot. That's how opposite it is here.

There is a funny farm (I know that's not politically correct, but that's what it is) near here. These mentally disabled people work on the farm—OK, it's a petting zoo. They clean things and feed animals. These men—they're mostly men—stand waiting for the five o'clock train every day.

One man rocks back and forth constantly, wagging his big body to and fro. He makes a hand gesture so the engineer will pull the whistle. He likes to say the word "Fruitcake!" really loud. Actually, he shouts it.

There's another man who doesn't stop talking. He repeats commercials aloud to himself. "Dial 1-800 . . . our lucky winners will get a free vacation . . . buy one get one free . . . for a limited time only . . . half off . . . sweet, delicious . . . cool, refreshing . . . act now . . . ," etc.

I wonder if his brain isn't a satellite dish, picking all this stuff out of the air and spewing it back. This is also the kind of shit that gets me depressed.

Are you there God? It's me, Dope Fiend.

Just try to find a used record store here. Just try to find a resale shop here. Just try to find a used-book store here. You want knickknacks? You want wicker knickknacks? You want doodads? Come in, come in.

One day a Swedish girl comes up to Auntie and me on the street. The girl has a wicker basket with her and she unfolds a blanket delicately to reveal . . . small stuffed puppy dogs. She's selling them.

"So cute, so cute," she says, beseechingly. To my horror, Auntie tells me to put a brown-and-white pup in her Nordstrom's bag.

There is a monastery near here, I learned recently while reading the local paper. Apparently a monk got hit riding his bicycle the other day. He got hit by a southbound train; he had headphones on and didn't hear the approach. He went flying into the street. You can see this— a flying monk, a twisted bike, the horrified onlookers trapped at the crossing in their BMWs and new Volkswagen Beetles.

After a month, Auntie hints that I may want to look for a job. There is a cute boy who works in this key shop. I decide to look for work in the key shop.

The key shop is called Stan the Key Man. It's a house that's been converted into a shop. When you step inside, you know this used to be a living room. There are tons of locks and keys on pegboard walls. Cute Boy says hello, may he help me, and I say yes, I'm looking for a job. He twitches and hesitates, thinking. Then, he finds a form for me to fill out.

I don't get the job at the key shop, but I've managed to give the cute boy my home telephone number. One day later he calls and nervously apologizes that Stan doesn't have openings. Cute Boy's voice is shaking, and that makes him even cuter.

"So are you new to town?" he asks.

"Yes, I am," I say.

"Have you been to the Spot Bowl?" he asks.

"No, I have not," I say.

"I can take you. They have cosmic bowling," he says.

"Far out," I say.

"What?"

"Cosmic," I say. "Intergalactic."

"Oh, yeah. Anyway . . ."

"Tomorrow," I say, wondering about my auntie in the other room watching *Matlock*. "Meet me at the 7-11 at seven."

"OK."

I hang up. I've always wanted to meet someone at the 7-11. Why has it taken this long?

That night there is a terrific thunderstorm. Power lines go down. There's a gas leak.

God says: I was just kidding.

Brian, his name is. Brian is about as smart and as dumb as I want him to be. He can't be any better looking. He's going back to school in the fall, to college downstate. Business major, but I can forgive him. Stan the Key Man is a summer job.

"It's not so bad," he says. "Sometimes I go out to replace locks on things. And you?"

And you.

"I'm visiting my auntie for the summer," I say, rubbing my arms unconsciously.

Dinky Hocker Shoots Smack.

Otherwise Known as Sheila the Whore.

We move on. We bowl. He drinks. I drink Cokes. I drink Cokes like Coke is it. I bum one of his cigarettes. I pull the city into my lungs and cough it back out.

I get home late and go inside with the taste of his mouth in mine. Marlboro and Trident Wintergreen. Auntie is up, like in the movies. We hear Brian's Camaro wheel out into the night. I walk soberly to the kitchen and pull a glass of water from the faucet.

"Good night, dear," Auntie says.

"Good night," I say.

I get a job in a local frame shop. I work with a woman, the owner. She's the color of an orangutan's butt from too many hours in the tanning salon. Hours pass and we do not talk. Auntie knows her. This is probably a favor. Probably, this woman knows about me.

And you.

Days collide. They stick together. They get mashed and whipped and served. Brian and I have sex in his car in some make-out woods someplace. It is hot backseat sex with his sweat dripping off his forehead into my eyes, the windows fogged. He knows more about me, but he'll never know enough.

I am sometimes asked by Auntie to think about the future. To think about *my* future.

"You're such a bright thing," Auntie says. "You can do whatever you set your mind to."

I'm asked to think about college. Specifically, the local community college. When the summer ends, Brian and I break up. Or I break him up. He thinks I'll be here waiting for him while he's at school banging freshman chicks. He's wrong. But I'm not returning his shirt. I like the smell of it. Of him.

I'm in a class. A philosophy class. Seems like the place to start. When you know nothing about anything besides Judy Blume, you gotta get a grip. You gotta take a step up.

Get up and get out.

I think Iggy Pop said that.

Halloween

U ncle Creepy walked into the fast-food restaurant. It was Halloween night, near two in the morning. He was on his way home from a party, a costume party, and suddenly he'd gotten the urge to have a slider. Maybe six of them; there was no telling. He pulled into the lot.

Inside, the place was bright white. It was white everywhere—the floors, the wall tiles, the ceiling, the lights. There was a short line. Some drunk guys with backwards baseball caps and five o'clock shadows were ordering food. When it was his turn to order, Uncle Creepy smiled, sickly, at the teen-age girl behind the counter and asked for a ten pack of burgers with fries.

"Anything to drink with that, sir?" she asked, eyeing him warily.

"Not unless you have any blood of newt or mole's bile," he said.

The girl rolled her eyes and gave the order to the cook. "Please step down."

Uncle Creepy moved to where the young men were gathered near the pick-up window using profanities. They must have been pretty drunk, he surmised, or else they would have recognized him by now. Out-of-towners, probably. But then, one of the boys, one with a VW hood ornament around his neck and sunglasses, pointed at him.

"Dudes, check it out! It's Uncle Creepy!" he said.

The others turned. There was a moment of silence, and then the three of them burst out laughing.

"Jesus, it's really him, man!"

"Hey, it's the Creep!"

"Dude, man, you gotta do that thing. Y'know," and the goateed one bared his teeth and gnarled his hands.

Uncle Creepy looked back to see how his order was doing.

"Oh, c'mon, man. Do it!"

"Yeah, do it, say 'Hello Kiddies!'"

Uncle Creepy looked at the kid, who was wearing Converse All-Stars, and gave him the finger.

A new wave of laughter rolled out of the boys. "Man, you just got flipped off by Uncle Creepy! Cool!"

"Hey man, why don't you ever read my letters on the air?" VW demanded.

"Yeah, and how come I never got that autographed photo you promised?" Goatee asked.

"You forgot to put the check in the envelope," Uncle Creepy said.

The kids laughed. "Is that makeup, or is that really your face?" Converse asked. Uncle Creepy stared at him with his bloodshot eyes.

Converse laughed nervously and jerked a thumb at Uncle Creepy. "Heh, heh, y'know what I like so much about Uncle Creepy is, he's so *eerie*."

"Yeah," Goatee rejoined, "and you know what I like so much about Cousin Eerie?"

"He's so CREEPY!" they all shouted.

Then their order was up. "Hey man, later days . . . keep chillin' . . . ride free, brother!" And the three of them left. Uncle Creepy saw them climb into a monster truck and peel out of sight, rap music blaring from the windows.

A minute later, a Mexican teenager pushed Uncle Creepy his bag of burgers. He had plastic fang teeth on and displayed them. Uncle Creepy grunted and went to a window booth.

Most of the tables were empty, as most everyone was getting their orders to go or was at the drive-through window.

After brushing some salt flecks to the floor, Uncle Creepy took out the ten small burgers and the bag of fries and positioned them in front of him. Paying no attention to the long-haired youth in a jean jacket, who was sitting in the next booth staring at him, he began to deliver the burgers to his mouth.

He knew it was going to happen, and finally it did: the youth started talking to him. At first he smiled, and then he chuckled, his fat cheeks nearly bursting, and then he said, "I'll be damned. You *are* Uncle Creepy."

Uncle Creepy looked up briefly at the kid and then dismissed him as irrelevant. The kid chuckled again.

"I grew up with you, man," he said.

"So why don't you move away from me now?" Uncle Creepy said.

"You're the shit, man."

"Cannabis is illegal in this state," Uncle Creepy said.

"Hey man, I heard you were a heroin addict. Is that true?"

"I heard your mother sucks cocks in hell," Uncle Creepy said. "I mean, *op-bop-bop* . . ."

"Man, you're just like on TV—totally rude."

"And you're just like most of my fans—totally brain-dead."

"Sorry, Uncle Creepy, you're not getting to me, man. I know it's an act—you're just in character now. Boy, you sure are dedicated."

"And you sure are annoying."

"Hey, can I get an autograph, dude? C'mon, what do you say?"

"The only thing that gets my signature is death certificates."

"Aw, c'mon, man."

"Get lost."

"All right, man," the kid said. "Well, party on."

"Burn in hell."

It was his standard dismissal.

By now, Uncle Creepy was halfway through his meal. The greasy patties were settling uneasily, like restless tadpoles, in his stomach. He was glad to be out of that suburb and away from all the rich kids. He had been well paid for his appearance at the twenty-first birthday party, and, as he had specifically outlined in his agreement with David's parents, they had provided him with a bottle of Maker's Mark. However, it probably wasn't helping his image any, playing the fool for a crowd of drunk college students.

Apart from that, all of his attempts at preying upon the cute vixens had fallen short. He had to face the facts—he wasn't as young or popular as he used to be. Maybe selling out as gruesomely as possible was his only option.

As he was pondering all this, the Black Widow walked in. It was just his luck. After studiously avoiding her for the last couple of years and declining any and all public appearances in which she too might participate, it was not amusing in the least that he should run into his horror-host archrival on Halloween, of all times.

Uncle Creepy immediately looked away when he recognized her, hoping in vain that she was just another teenager in one of a thousand copycat costumes (a manner in which his own image was also likely emulated, though probably not to such a frequent degree). She had seen him too, and, he noticed, she wore a demonic smile laden with sadistic intimations that turned up her blood-red lips.

The Widow had her back to Uncle Creepy now and was placing her order. She was dressed in the same garb she always wore on her hit program *Horrorshow*—a long black dress, low-cut in the fashion of German beer waitresses; long black hair falling straight past her milk-white shoulders; eyes heavily shaded with mascara; long fake eyelashes; high heels. Her hips and bosom threw themselves at the world. The Widow emanated darkness, death, mystery, and, above all, sex.

Uncle Creepy began nervously eating his french fries, dipping them rapidly in the mound of ketchup he had squeezed onto his tray. He felt that he should just get up and leave, but also that this would be perceived as a sign of weakness. No, he must remain, and remain, above all, dignified.

After posing for a few pictures and signing a few autographs for the drunken monsters standing in line, the Widow crossed over to where Uncle Creepy sat staring at the moving traffic and chewing slowly.

"Well, well," the Widow said. "All sorts of vermin crawling out from beneath rocks tonight."

Turning his weathered old eyes upon the striking form of the Widow, who stood holding a tray of food aloft, Uncle Creepy said, "Better take it easy on the fries, my dear. It seems you've gained recently."

"Ha!" said the Widow, jumping into the seat across from him, "at least I don't look like I crawled out of a crypt!"

"Then my dearie, you seem to have completely and utterly missed the point."

"Still giving lessons, old man?"

"You could stand some."

"What? So my show could take a dive like yours? Huh!"

"The only reason *Horrible* does well is because lonely boys need to masturbate to your mammaries."

At this, the Widow smiled.

"I guess chicken-choking is better than chicken-throwing, which is all your show offers for amusement."

At this, Uncle Creepy's blood pressure soared. He eyes bugged out and a vein stood on his forehead.

"Harlot!" he growled.

"Has-been!"

"Tramp!"

"Turkey!"

"Strumpet!"

"Sell-out!"

It ended there. Uncle Creepy's withered heart was creaking noisily in his bony chest. His eyes shot arrows across the table of junk food. The Widow laughed and nibbled at her fries, shaking her head.

"So where were you tonight? At a child's birthday party?"

Uncle Creepy swallowed hard. He almost gagged. Finally, he coughed the food out into a napkin. "Out," he said.

"Well then, you must have missed my two-hour Halloween extravaganza on *Horrorshow*. We played *Mutant Mantis, The Snake People,* and *Corpse Walkers from Planet L.*"

That last title struck a nerve. It was obvious that she knew he'd been trying unsuccessfully to buy *Corpse Walkers* from Watershed Productions, and that his station, WZZD, didn't have the finances to procure it.

"And I'll bet you peppered your commentaries liberally with Uncle Creepy standbys, as usual." he said.

"Oh no," the Widow laughed, "you're much too dull. Too obvious and hackneyed. My viewers have *minds*, remember?"

Uncle Creepy was touched off, as if his head was a bottle rocket. He pointed across the table at his slanderer.

"Vile Demon-Wench of the Black Pit!" he said.

"Sordid Curmudgeon of the Lost Lagoon!" the Widow returned.

"Whore of Abomination Alley!"

"Lizard of Putrid Defamation!"

"Abortion of the Black Castle!"

"Gnarled Geriatric of the Place Too Evil to Name!"

They were both getting hoarse. Uncle Creepy stood up on his tired feet and waved the Widow aside like a halo of flies, but she came after him from behind like a specter. Before he could turn to face her, she had raked her long nails across his leathery face. Blood ran from her fingertips and made large droplets on the stark white floor.

The Widow laughed maniacally. "Cheer up, you'll die soon!" she crowed.

Too astonished to react, Uncle Creepy stood transfixed as the Widow made her exit from the opposite side of the restaurant. Several people surrounded Uncle Creepy moments later, asking him if he was all right. The manager of Burger World, wearing a headset and baseball cap, was dabbing at Uncle Creepy's cheek with a napkin and asking him if he should call the police.

Uncle Creepy grabbed the napkin from the manager and furiously threw it to the floor. He stared at the vanished apparition of the Widow and cursed.

He didn't need to taste it.

The blood was fake.

Moiré Patterns

Life begins here.

I don't remember the carrying in of the Zenith; I'm not sure if it was delivered or what. Suddenly it's there in the living room, situated near the windows.

It's chrome, mirrored on all sides. It's like a spaceship, an exotic passageway to other dimensions. I'm up early one weekend morning, before my parents, watching these three men. The men are together in everything they do—riding horses, getting thrown into prison, running through doorways. The men are often hurting each other—pulling teeth out with pliers, yanking hair, poking eyes. I suspect this is old; that the things these people are doing happened a long time ago. It seems like I'm visiting that time, though; it's like I'm there. If I make cups of my hands and blind the sides of my eyes, I'm almost completely there. The only things missing are smells and touches. Otherwise, I have time-traveled with this giant silvery orb in front of me.

One day my mother, my sister, and I are together watching TV. A cartoon is on, one that I like a lot—*Quick Draw McGraw*. Quick Draw has a persona he changes into called "El Kabong." El Kabong has a Zorro-type mask, a cape, and a guitar that he uses to club evildoers over the head with. When he performs this last action, he yells *"El Kabong!"*

I love this show, especially when he yells his trademark line.

For some reason, my mother has purchased guitars for my sister and me. Lisa has a big yellow acoustic and I've got a ukulele. Neither of us can play these things, but we like to hold them. On this one particular day, I'm holding my ukulele while watching this cartoon. My mother and I are on the couch and my sister is sitting on the floor in front of us. At a critical part of the show, the part where El Kabong is smashing his guitar on the heads of others, I have a break with reality or something. I have no other explanation for what I do next: without warning or provocation, I lift up my ukulele in front of my mother and bring it crashing down on my sister's head while saying—what else?—*EL KABONG*!!!!

The ukulele shatters; my sister cries out; my mother smacks me.

Ernie and Bert are talking. Bert decides to make a peanut-butter sandwich. I see Bert eating the sandwich. Suddenly, I want a peanut-butter sandwich. My mom agrees to make me one.

General Hospital. One Life to Live. Love American Style. Little House on the Prairie. The Waltons. I fall asleep to the wah-wah song that informs me that my mother is spending time with Jim Rockford.

Batman, the '60s TV show, is on. My heart begins to race with pure adrenaline caused by the intro music. Within minutes, I am Batman. I am jumping off the couch with a blue bath towel pinned around my neck, punching out leather-capped flunkies.

Sonny and Cher's variety show is on. There is a cartoon interlude. A cave girl is introduced. Her name is "Furl." Furl is very pretty. I have an erection. I am in love with Furl.

Surf forward three years.

Steve Austin. A man barely alive. *Gentlemen, we have the technology.* I am the Six Million Dollar Man, age seven. I act out the beginning rocket-ship crash in a chair on the patio. I make rumbling noises and quaking motions and eventually fall down on the ground, at which point I will be taken away to be "rebuilt." I call my mother out to witness this one-act play. I think it's brilliant.

We're getting moiré patterns on the TV. My father is trying to fix this. His solution, like all of his around-the-house solutions, is jury-rigged. He is attaching huge flags of aluminum foil to the rabbit ears. This never works, of course, but it allows him to do something. I have been called downstairs from my room by his shouting: "Come down here! Look at this!"

I stand in the living room, where my father is positioning the antennas this way and that, twisting the foil as tight as he can make it. On the TV, there are some native African people, apparently building homes out of clay.

"Look at 'em," my father says. "They're actually mixing the mud with cow dung!"

This is why I am never enthused when I am called to witness something on the TV. Last time I ended up watching alligators mating.

There's a party at the house. People are drinking. I am upstairs in my parents' bedroom (the quietest room in the house). I can't sleep because of the noise downstairs. I turn on the black-and-white and watch Ned Beatty getting pushed through mud, in long underwear, in a forest. He's scared. I have never seen a man that scared before. This is unsettling.

I'm on the couch with a fever in the living room. It's late on a Saturday night. My mother is watching a Jodie Foster movie: *The Little Girl Who Lives Down the Lane*. Jodie Foster is a creepy little girl. Martin Sheen is a creepy detective. The girl has buried her father beneath the house.

Saturday morning is Christmastime each week. *Super Friends, Electra Woman and Dyna Girl, Shazam*. Oh mighty *Isis*. I drink the sucrose milk from my cereal dish. Come to the Honeycomb Hideout.

My dad is Barney Miller. My dad is Archie Bunker. My dad is Louie from *Taxi*.

Gunshots. Reagan goes down. Trench coats push him violently into a limo.

Twilight Zone, The Honeymooners, Saturday Night Live, Late Night with David Letterman. Tylenol murders. Empire Carpet commercials. DeVry. Victory Auto Wreckers. *That car is worth money*. Surf forward.

The movie *Halloween* is on TV. Holy shit. Holy freaking shit. Surf forward.

Now for something completely different.

I am drunk for the first time in my life. Screwdrivers. I'm sixteen, and I'm puking my eyes out. It's a Saturday afternoon. I return home as my dad is bringing in a new TV. He won a trifecta at the horse track. This is a pattern. New appliances arrive in the house when he wins trifectas. I am supposed to be excited by the TV. I go upstairs and pass out on the bed.

There is a Kentucky Derby party at the house. Everyone's standing around the basement with Mint Juleps and bottled beer. The chrome Zenith remote is busted. To change channels, you have to jingle a set of car keys. No one knows why this has the magic ability to change the station. The race is on. As the horses near the finish line, the TV becomes a field of white noise.

Surf forward four years.

President Bush is explaining how ruthlessly Kuwait has been trampled and how he hopes for a "new world peace." There are times when it looks like a smile is creeping onto his face but, just as quickly, it disappears, and I am only looking at his cold, robotic eyes, unsure whether I detected anything at all.

At night my friends and I gather in the basement around the TV, drinking beers. We're in college. There is talk of moving to Amsterdam. Fuck America.

I am not a number. I'm a free man!

Chicago floods. L.A. burns. O. J. runs.

I order a videotape of a local director's low-budget horror movie, *Mummy AD.* He calls occasionally to let me know of his latest releases, dates when he will be interviewed on TV. One day I run into him at a horror-memorabilia store opening. He has a video camera with him and is wearing a rubber monster glove. He films his hand choking me.

Surf forward three months. I get a call informing me that the choking sequence may be shown on *The Daily Show* on Comedy Central. My brother tapes it. A week later I see myself on TV, getting mock-strangled by a monster hand.

I am pixels. I am photons.

I am light.

The Wall

I t happens overnight, or seems to.

When Packer-Shore sells our retirement community to Spetz Development, I read about the deal in our newsletter, *The Daily Sunshine*. Not two days after the hand-off is official, a man in a suit comes to our door. He has jet-black hair, a doll's head and a taped-on smile. He could be forty; he could be twenty-five.

He introduces himself as Jim Score, CEO of Spetz, says he's making the rounds of the community, meeting the residents and taking an informal survey to see if folks are satisfied with the present security in our neighborhood or if they'd welcome an adjustment on that front.

"We're testing the waters, in case we decide to go out to bid," Score says. "I'm letting everybody know that at Spetz, your safety and security are our number one priority. Can I put you down as an interested party for enhanced safety?"

"How much will this increase our association fees?" I ask.

"Oh, nothing. Absolutely nothing. This would be done on Spetz's dime, completely."

"Well, I'm not sure it's needed. Things seem pretty secure to me."

"Fair enough," Score says. "At present that may be true, but with an eye to the future, the way the population is growing over in Arbor Heights, that could change. We all might be glad we took steps sooner rather than later. An effective security team in place early would help to curb certain undesirable elements from making criminal overtures in WellSprings. I've already spoken to several of your neighbors—Candy Dimond, Chad Blackwell and Norv Davis, and they've all signaled interest in this initiative."

To me this added security will be a waste of money, like buying a padlock you intend on keeping in a junk drawer, so I'm not inclined to "signal interest," but since it's not my money, and I have a dinner plate cooling in the dining room, I tell Score that it can't hurt, go ahead and put me down.

"Thanks, Mr. Fincher," he says, his smile growing exponentially. "Do let me know if there's anything I can do for you." He hands me his business card and bids me good day. He goes down the walk to a gleaming black Cadillac with the vanity plate **SPETZ 1** on it.

A week later I'm on the nine hole with my buddies Todd and Ollie, and we see a trio of men in mud-grey uniforms strolling along the perimeter of the course. Their aviators mirror the sun as they pause to observe our round.

Todd tees off into the brush.

"Goddamn it," he says. "I can't play with an audience watching!"

He stands pat and stares back at the men until they finally resume their walk.

"Who are those guys?" Ollie says. I'm wondering that myself, but I think I know.

"That's the new security," Todd says, taking a mulligan on the swing and grabbing another ball. "I saw them over at the gate house the other day. They had some vans there unloading equipment."

"What kind of equipment?"

"I don't know . . . High-tech gadgets and such. Satellite dishes . . . Who knows?"

"Oh yeah, I heard about that. Frieda told me a guy came to the house and surveyed her about security," Ollie says.

"We're not paying for it. That's what the paper said," Todd says.

"So they say. But I betcha there'll be some new fee. They'll finance this from our pockets somehow," I say, regretting giving Score my consent.

A couple days after our golf game, I'm going out to the Meier with Mel and we pass by the gatehouse and see some of the equipment Todd referred to. There look to be three antenna-type things on the roof, a couple satellite dishes, a new steel door and windows replaced with tinted stuff.

We roll by slowly, our eyeballs capturing this in snapshots.

"What are they up to here?"

"That must be Kleig security," Mel says. "Phyllis and I saw some of the men over at the Rec Center when the girls and I had sewing class."

I stomp on the gas and take our white-fenced, curvy road at a speed not meant for it.

"Score didn't say anything about equipment," I say. "Or anything about outfitting our gate house to look like an Army command post."

"Looks like they're going to have people in it, huh?" Mel says.

"I can't imagine why," I said. "What were they doing over at the Rec Center?"

"I don't know. We just saw them walking along the pool watching people swim and then later on they were talking to Kurt Winter. He was taking them around with a set of keys. Kathy mentioned seeing a bunch of the security guys over at Nikko's having lunch. She said they looked like a sullen bunch."

Down at the Center Bar on Sunday with Todd and Ollie, having our usual black and tans and watching the Bears lose, I notice a small black tube. It's high up in the corner and when I get up to hit the head, it follows me, or seems to.

When I finish business I ask Frenchy, the bartender what that thing is up in the corner. Frenchy frowns and squeezes a rag out in the sink.

"Camera," he says sourly. "The new security talked to Doyle, and he let them put it in. Don't know what interest it is to anyone to watch a fella pour drinks and watch others drink them, but then I ain't the boss . . ."

"That pick up sound?" Todd asks.

"Not as far as I'm aware… But you know, I didn't think to ask."

"Doyle in?" I say. I want to talk to that Irish bastard right now.

"On vacation," Frenchy says. "Wife and him on a month-long cruise."

"I'll speak to him when he gets back," I say.

"I'll come with ya," Todd says.

Ollie's got his head in the game and doesn't seem to have heard much of this. He cries out when our QB almost gets his head torn off and used as a hood ornament. I finish up my beer and try to enjoy the game, but I can't keep my eye off the eye. Frenchy seems sorry about it, but it isn't his fault. Instead of finishing out the game, when half time comes, I tell the fellas I'm out of here.

"Yeah, I think I'll do the same," Todd says.

"You guys are going?" Ollie says. "You're not gonna stay and watch the rest of the game?"

"Not when the game is watching *us*," I say, pointing to the camera.

From what Mel and I hear, people are divided over the new security. Some find comfort in those men with the mud-grey uniforms. They buy Score's theory that one day Arbor Heights' population is going to overflow with gangs and then we'll see police blotters containing stories about TVs stolen in WellSprings. Others, like me, Mel and Todd are starting to feel hemmed in.

When I tell my ex-military neighbor Chad about the changes we're seeing, he agrees that it seems unnecessary, a bit overkill.

"Anybody come for my TV, they'll have to speak to my Glock or my Luger . . . I'm not worried about that. I may be old but I can still pull a trigger."

When I tell him about the camera in the bar, he doesn't see the harm. Says there are cameras everywhere these days.

"Yeah, but does anybody watch them? Not unless something happens. I get the feeling there's somebody *watching* us over there."

Chad shrugs and whips open a leaf bag. "I wouldn't worry about it," he says. "Probably just a deterrent."

Next weekend Mel and I go out to Prairie Forks to visit our daughter Susie's family, and we get back after nine. As we get close to the gatehouse, I see something new—a row of large cannon-shaped lights slashing down at the entrance and an actual gate blocking the way.

"What the shit is this?" I say, not believing my eyes. I pull close to the guardhouse as far as I can go and a black Plexiglas window slides to the side, revealing a young man with a severe buzz cut.

"Good evening Mr. Fincher," the young man says, looking at a monitor just out of view. "Should I check you in for the evening?"

My mouth will hardly work to form words.

"Check in? *What*? What's this gate for?"

"It's just for after sundown, sir," the guard says. "Just a precaution. If we know your vehicle will be here for the night then we'll know to question the driver should it attempt to leave later."

Mel has the same rage going as I do. She leans over to square eyes with the kid.

"No one is going to take our car," she says.

"Great, so I'll just check you in for the night then."

"That's not what I meant," Mel snips. "No one is going to *steal* the car."

"No check in is needed. Put us down as 'questionable,'" I say. "Now lift this gate!"

"Sir, the gate is just for your safety."

"The hell it is," I say. As soon as it ratchets up, I pull through, cursing.

"Well, that's the limit," Mel says. "I didn't hear anything about this. What do we need a gate for?"

"We *don't*."

The next morning I'm working on an email to Score, telling him what I think of this new gate, when Mel comes back from sewing class.

"Back so soon?"

"You're not going to believe this," Mel says. "They cancelled my class!"

"Rain check for another day?"

"No, I mean they *cancelled* it. In fact, they said that all classes are cancelled for the immediate future while they do some reorganization."

"Getting your money back?"

"Yes, but that's not the point . . . We like our instructor, Kira. We were in the middle of a project! We complained at the front desk, but the girl there didn't know anything. She just said the only class available at this time was this."

Mel shows me a flyer for a one day exclusive event called *Safe and Secure—Protecting Home and Family*. At the bottom there's a photo of the doll-headed Score smiling so wide his face could split. The flyer lists things that will be covered in the session including safety in the home, at the gym, in the car, online and in the backyard. It seems like ten bags of bullshit in a two-pound bag.

"Did anyone sign up?"

"We all signed up just to see what it's about," Mel says.

"You did *what*?"

"We want to find out what these people are up to. We'll meet them on their own turf if we have to." Mel is flushed she's so fired up.

"When is this thing?"

"Next Thursday."

"You're not going."

"Why not?"

"It's brainwashing, that's why."

"But all the girls are going. We want to see what it's about."

"No further discussion," I say firmly. "You're staying here."

Thursday comes and goes and we hear from some of our friends, Ollie and his wife Frieda and Cal Johnson and his wife Tammy. They say they went in skeptical of the changes, but Score convinced them what's going on is for everyone's benefit. It's just what I thought would happen. Score is gassing everybody with his flowery talk.

At poker on Friday night, Ollie mentions the wall.

"What wall?"

"They want to put an eight foot cinder block wall around the perimeter," he says.

"What in hell for?"

"To keep out the undesirables," Ollie says. "Thugs. The criminal element."

"You see any crime here?" I say, incredulous.

"We're preparing for the future."

"First the new security personnel, then cameras watching us, then a gate and now a *wall*? This is out of hand," I say. "When's it going to stop?"

"No, really," Ollie says, turning the river card, a three. No help. "He showed us the stats. We don't do this now and one day we'll be overrun. They're already seeing some gang graffiti on the post office wall downtown."

Then Ollie goes on to tell us Score has another proposal in the offing to allow residents to have outside visitors on designated holidays only as well as five additional, pre-arranged days a year.

"Where did you hear about that?"

"*Daily Sunshine*."

I realize I haven't seen the paper lately.

I'm sending another email.

The next day the doorbell rings. It's a man in a blue suit with a gold tag on his breast pocket that IDs him as a Spetz employee.

"Yes?"

"Good day Mr. Fincher," the guy says, another young/old type. "I'm collecting signatures for the Community Defense Project Proposal."

"The *what*?"

"Perhaps you've heard there's an initiative to construct a barrier?"

"Yes, I did hear," I say. "And I think it's a bunch of horseshit."

"It's a *decorative* barrier," the man says. "It serves to both protect and beautify the community as well as to reduce noise from the highway."

"There *is* no noise from the highway," I say. "Stand in the yard out back a minute and tell me you can hear a single car."

"While you may not have a noise problem, sir, there are others in the community who—"

"I'm not signing it!"

"It's for the community interest."

I slam the door shut.

I don't consider what effect this act of civil disobedience may have, but the following day I start to find out.

Kleig men start driving by at all hours, sometimes stopping to stare at the house.

Next thing is I get a violation notice in the mail for a tree I planted in the backyard last spring. The three foot high Kwanzan Cherry is not on the list of "approved trees" for our community. A lengthy note attached to the bill informs me that application for tree approval can be submitted, but any adjacent neighbors must agree to the planting in a sworn affidavit. Since appropriate registrations have not been met,

I owe two hundred dollars, payable in ten days or it goes up to three hundred.

Mel, already on edge with the men staring at the house, urges me to comply, but I'm not having any of it. I tear the bill in two. I do this on the doorstep in full view of the Kleig men idling on the curb.

This action perhaps causes the next—I'm cited for an "improper stone" on the front lawn. This is a flat, circular stone with our last name etched into it and is apparently not "code-approved." Another bill is attached for having an "animal-themed lawn ornament" (a tiny ceramic rabbit) on display. Both violations are for seventy-five dollars apiece.

These bills are also shredded, but this time done so on top of a Kleig vehicle.

The man drives off and nearly over my foot.

The next day I'm back from the grocery and find Mel having coffee in the breakfast nook with Jim Score. It's like discovering a rattlesnake on the linoleum. Mel rises quickly to calm me. She says she invited Mr. Score over so we might work out a reasonable agreement to the fine business.

"—and I was telling your lovely wife, Mr. Fincher, that we are certainly willing to disregard the fines in question if we could only obtain your compliance and consent on our building project."

"The wall," I say.

"An ugly term. Most ugly. I don't like *barrier* either. I prefer to call it a *separator*. Or landscape line. Much better, don't you think?"

"Eight meters of cinder block is not a line," I practically spit. "It's a *wall*. I refuse to sign any consent form and what's more, you can take your violation notices and put them where the sun don't shine. Now please, remove yourself, sir. You are intruding in my home."

This of course, upsets Mel to no end. Here she thought she was making headway with Score, and now I've dashed the whole thing to pieces.

"We'll consider your offer, of course, Mr. Score," Mel says as he rises and takes his leather trench coat off the back of the chair.

"We'll do no such thing," I say through my teeth.

Score leaves, careful not to brush into me on his way out. When he's gone, Mel and I have one of the biggest arguments of our thirty-four year marriage. The upshot of it is, I won't be blackmailed into signing something I don't believe in.

"Well then just pay the stupid fines," Mel says. "Honey, this is where we *live* . . . We can't be at odds with the community."

After some time and considerable back and forth, I agree to this since it's the wall I'm really against. The fines are paid, the stone, tree and rabbit removed. The Kleig men disappear and for a little while, we're left alone.

Then one Monday afternoon I get a call from Frenchy at Center Bar. He says I won the drawing for the free dinner for two at Nikko's, can I come down to collect?

I say sure I'll be right down.

But when I arrive at the bar, I have to knock on the glass since the door has a sign that says it's closed. Frenchy opens up but doesn't look like a guy about to give another guy a prize. In fact, it looks the opposite. He takes me into the back room where I supposedly need to sign something, and he's pushed aside by two Kleig men who are wearing ski masks. One of the men has a German shepherd on a chain, and it doesn't look too friendly.

When they move to restrain me, I try to get a lick in on the smaller one, but I'm brought down by a truncheon strike to the back of my knees. My hands are wrenched behind my back and cuffed tightly. I'm blindfolded and a rag is stuck in my mouth as I'm ushered out the back way and thrust violently in a vehicle.

I'm told that sure as Christmas is December 25th, I will sign a document sanctioning the wall-building. I will start abiding by the code. I will not get in the way of the common interest.

After several dizzying turns, the cuffs are removed along with the blindfold and mouth rag, and I'm deposited roughly onto the asphalt parking lot in back of the driving range. No one is out today with the blustery weather.

Just as I'm straightening up, a Cadillac with the plate **Spetz 1** pulls up and stops.

Score's inside with an attractive, empty-eyed blonde. Both are dressed for church, or dressed up anyway. "Sort of a bad day for the range, wouldn't you say?" Score says, smiling across the blonde. "But you know, I'm glad I ran into you Mr. Fincher . . . I was wondering if you'd had any more thoughts about the separator?"

"Hadn't really thought of it," I say.

"That's a shame. In any case, we obtained the needed amount of signatures, so yours won't be necessary. Nonetheless, in appreciation of your input, we've decided to waive those fines we discussed earlier. Your money will be returned and your lawn offenses, well, the way we figure it, everyone's entitled to a little individuality now and then."

"So kind of you."

"I hope you come to appreciate the separator. I hope you'll find it makes a more cohesive community in the end—one big safe and happy family. Good day, Mr. Fincher. Be seeing you."

With a smile and an odd salute, Score drills up his automatic window and tears off the lot and down the curvy lane bordered by white picket fence, the same fence Mel and I dreamed of having one day. It was a factor, one of many, that convinced us that WellSprings was the place for us to live out our golden years.

But looking at the fence on this damp and windy day, I don't see the allure any more. I see something else.

On the hill are day laborers, their heads bowed to the falling rain, with pick axes and shovels going at the dirt.

Oblivious to me, they're bent in repetitive motion, standing near a battered red pickup truck beside an expressway that doesn't make a sound.

Modern Carnivores

Last week had been Allen's week. Craig Spiceland was sitting on the sofa, feet propped on the water-warped coffee table separating him from the game show on TV. It was Sunday and it was his week.

Macaroni & cheese dinners served as life-support in times of low food; ever since Allen's sister Jane got a job with Kraft, their apartment was always crowded with cheese and snack products. But real sustenance was necessary, and since what little income they had was usually spent on beer, they had agreed to the creed: *Food is out there, you just have to take it.*

Craig pasted a cracker with a thick coating of processed cheese, which he then expertly devoured in a single chomp. On the TV, contestants were obediently following the crazy rules of *Beat the Dealer*. Bob Coin, the host of the show, had porcelain-white teeth. A grin was stamped permanently on his face.

In the adjoining kitchenette, Allen looked up from his philosophy textbook and asked Craig if he couldn't turn down the show while he was trying to read.

"Screw you, man. You realize I'm gonna make us rich?" Craig said through a mouthful of crackers.

"Not on that side of the screen you're not," Allen said. "Give me some of those cheesy snack things."

Craig whipped a plastic-wrapped preservative bomb in the general direction of Allen's head. When he ducked, his *Speed Racer* coffee mug overturned on the table.

"Jesus!" Allen said. "You look inside that white thing over there called a refrigerator lately? It's empty and it's your turn to make a killing. Why don't you grab us some grub while you're not busy? We can't live out of those Kraft boxes, you know . . ."

When the show went to commercial, Craig clicked the TV off.

"Maybe I'll trap some rats and serve stew tonight," he said, pulling on his boots.

"Do what ya gotta do, just don't come back empty-handed," Allen said as Craig walked out the door.

They had been living out of boxes and cans for years, it seemed. Jane would come over once a month with a suitcase full of Kraft products, all smiles. She had a nice smile. Good teeth. Sometimes she'd bring a bottle of something with her and keep them up all night with stories. She seemed to be reliving her college experience when she came by. Looking at her, you would probably guess she was still in college, but she was already six years out. Thinking about her as he walked, Craig remembered how nice it was to see a woman in their apartment; the place was a lot less depressing in her company.

Craig stopped at a bench near Drox Park and lit a cigarette, thinking over the previous methods he and Allen had used to keep their stomachs full over the past two school years. A check from home would sometimes come, but usually they were all broke after book and rent payments. Food had to be obtained for little or close to nothing. Barry had it easy his weeks. His rich girlfriend Charlotte would often pay for his kill, which wasn't really considered a kill because the money was earned and coupons were used—a sacrilege in the highest form in Allen's view. Barry would walk in and drop a bag of groceries down like it was Saturday morning and Mom had just come home from the market. Allen and Craig never complained though, as there was always more than an ample amount of food for all of them.

For Allen and Craig though, food was always to be obtained in the most bizarre and illegal ways. There was a certain style to it. Nutrition didn't count, weight did. It was a competitive sport between them.

Craig's mind wandered like a hummingbird over flowers, resting on one occasion when, way back in fall, Allen had stuffed steaks down the arm holes of his jacket and nonchalantly bought a pack of thirty-five cent gum, the receipt for which he happily brandished when he returned. On another occasion, he spotted a campus delivery truck with an open door and a nonexistent driver, a killing that netted them foodstuffs for close to a month. Craig thought they would be lucky if they made it through another year with a clean record. He exhaled a cloud of smoke and tightened his jacket around his famished-looking body. It was starting to rain. Great time for it too, he thought.

The hunt always began a few days in advance, inside the mind. Craig had a few ideas, all illegal. Who's to blame him though? he thought. He said on more than one occasion that if given a choice, he'd kill and cook his own food rather than pay for some processed shit from some factory where vermin prey on hot dogs and frozen dinners. He and Allen felt little remorse for their exploits.

"It's a goddamn need for christsakes," Craig explained on one not-so-sober evening. "Why should I feel bad about satisfying a physical need? I woke up yesterday in this society and they want me to pay for food. I'm a hunter, dammit, in a so-called civilized country with too many people in it. I don't know these people I steal from or if I chose to, those people I'd be shopping with. Why should I care?"

Craig's cigarette had gone out in the rain and he bent over to relight it. Little tremors danced in his stomach. After a few moments, he stood up and hunched his back against the wind and headed toward Kroag's Market. The path ahead was lined with berry bushes and wide-brimmed trees. Craig imagined himself scouring the underbrush for tasty roots, feeling the wet soil on his bare feet. He tapped his index finger against his teeth. Wouldn't last a day, he thought, and continued his daydream. The air was humid and a steady drizzle fell from the gods who were coughing up there with all that pollution.

Craig crossed the puddled parking lot to Kroag's and felt the cold, filtered air come at him as the electronic door wheezed shut. A walk around would give him courage, he knew.

Glazed donuts stared through cellophane window boxes. Slabs of meat were being weighed and priced electronically. Water had gone through a sugared process in a factory to be labeled Coca-Cola. Cheese and cow meat had found themselves an unlikely combination called pizza. Acned stock boys fed the shelves, bringing the plant and animal kingdom to the fingertips of the masses.

Craig had a mouthful of saliva. He was ready.

He went to an open check out aisle, bought a magazine with planets on the cover and walked outside where he donned a faded orange smock he had found at a resale shop recently. He patted his hair back and waited. A few minutes later, he found what he was looking for—a woman hurrying to place her groceries in the trunk of her car in the rain.

Craig trotted up behind her and asked in his most courteous voice: "Can I help you with those, Ma'am?"

The woman's face was a river of blue and red make-up. "No, that's just—" Her assertion that she was perfectly capable of loading her own groceries was cut short when she realized that the cart boy wasn't loading the bags—he was taking them out.

"Hey! What do you think—?"

With two large hands clenching a stuffed bag, Craig cut across the lot, heart pounding, shoes thumping into asphalt puddles, until he was near the railroad tracks which would take him most of the way home.

During the abrupt encounter, Craig thought he had glimpsed sirloin. When he was safely out of danger, he crept beneath a tree and affirmed his suspicion.

He had made a good kill.

There was pride in it.

Tonight there would be meat.

Government Psychic

I was sent to get the word on the government psychic. The postcard from my editor, Damon, gave me the address of an H. R. Wilson in Sable County, Florida.

I called up the airline and booked a first-class ticket for Saturday. I didn't bother scheduling the interview, figuring that, since H. R. was psychic, he'd know I was coming. That gave me exactly one day to do background at the Weston Library. I had to find out all I could about this Wilson character, since my motto was the same as that of the Boy Scouts of America: Be Prepared.

After a lingering lunch at the Flying Fish restaurant, I entered the mighty library, threw down my mermaid notebook, blank index cards, and retractable pen, and set to work. After two hours in the periodicals room winding through years of microfiche, I had five or so pages devoted to this reputed spoon-bending, pet-finding, ghost-hunting, armament-detecting, mind-reading government employee.

He seemed like an interesting guy.

On Saturday morning I was at Midway Airport. There had been a bomb scare not long before, so security was extra-tight. After having my Voc-Sens 2000 voice machine scoured for fifteen minutes by x-ray attendants, I was released into the confines of the aircraft, which had been painted as a likeness of Shamu the whale.

During the trip down, I had an hour-long discussion about wrist-watches with the passenger on my left. Delbert Humes was traveling to Florida for the purpose of attending a wristwatch convention. He modeled his gold-plated, multi-time-dimensional, glow-in-the-dark, waterproof, shockproof, James Bond watch for me. "It tells time, too," Delbert joked. My Mickey Mouse was no match for it. Once I managed to break free of this dead-end discussion, I stared at a William Saroyan book until my eyes started to ache.

And then I was in Florida, land of the orange, the dog track, and the handgun. Wilson lived not far from Miami, where he worked in a plain brown building devoted almost entirely to motor-vehicle licensing.

After checking into a one-night fleabag motel, I ate lunch at a place called Wolfies, which contained 99.9 percent people with white hair—even the waitresses. But the breaded shrimp and lemonade were excel-lent, and afterward I was ready to take a cab to the DMV.

En route, my Cuban cabbie pointed out all the sights—the cocaine wharf, the jai alai joint, the X-rated movie theaters, and the blood bank where the homeless people lined up to give blood. When we stopped at a traffic light, a prostitute climbed into the pickup truck ahead of us.

"This really seems like a family town," I said.

I twisted my head at the rows of rickety houses that lined the street we were on.

"Why are the houses on stilts?" I asked.

"Termites," the cabbie said. "Once you get them, you can't get rid of them."

And then we were there. The parking lot was full; apparently Saturday was the day people remembered that they owned cars, or maybe it was the only day that the licensing station was open. I paid the cabbie and hot-footed it across the melting parking lot. Inside the DMV, it was jam-packed. All around the room stood the an-gry, the non-English-speaking, the visually impaired, the parents of screaming children. It was like entering Saigon at the end of the Vietnam War.

I marched straight up to the old, blue-suited wizard at the informa-tion desk and asked him where I could find Wilson. The coot laughed and pointed to a doorway that was partially blocked by a standing line.

"Carnival Boy's over there!" he said. "But he might be on lunch."

I went over to the indicated door. To get to it, I had to step through the long line of people who were waiting to find out they'd forgotten a form or two that was required in order to get anything done. As I attempted to break through this line, a handbag came flying at my head.

"Stupido! Go to end. We wait long time!"

I looked into the pinched face of a squat woman.

"I'm just trying to get across!" I said, pointing to the door.

I got another handbag from the woman—this time, to the kidney.

"Go to back!" the woman said.

I felt that now was the time to say something crazy in Spanish on purpose.

"Vamos a la playa!" I shouted, *"y nadir en la aqua!"*

The woman looked at me like I was insane. I used the distraction to hop past her and bang on the plain blue door.

"Who is it?" a voice asked from inside. The door opened and a long-haired, goateed guy appeared. He was forty or so, skinny, balding, with a sharp nose and blue eyes. He was wearing an ELO shirt, purple Jolly Roger beach shorts, and Spiderman aqua socks.

"You mean you didn't know?" I asked.

"Oh, I did, it's just a habit. You know, like saying hello."

"Hello," I said.

"Hi, um . . . can I help you?"

I passed Wilson my card. Wilson looked at it and passed it back.

"What does it mean?"

"You mean even you haven't heard of *Inkvine*?"

"Frankly, no. What is it?"

"It's the magazine I work for. You're interview number twenty-one."

"Hmmm . . . lucky me. Well, I'm in the middle of lunch, but if you can wait until I finish my tuna sandwich, I'll be happy to answer your questions."

"Sure. Don't mind me," I said, walking in and surveying the place. The office was small, but its space was well-used. There were hanging plants, a stereo and TV, a microwave, a metal desk, a file cabinet, a closet, a waterbed, a video library, and a huge poster of Farrah Fawcett.

Wilson motioned for me to sit on a small yellow-and-white chair.

"This is some place," I said.

"Yeah. The Feds pretty much let me do what I want, so long as I give them what I got on time."

I set the voice recorder in motion.

"Bother you?" I asked.

"No, but it *bugs* me. Get it?"

If there's anything I hate, it's being a pun victim. I took out my mermaid notebook and drew a picture of somebody's head exploding.

"So," I said, "what do you give them?"

Wilson munched down the rest of his sandwich, swigged the last of his Kayo, and said, "Information. I look into the minds of foreign heads of state, into war zones, riots, anything security-related."

"And are you good at what you do?"

"Sure. There've been stories on me; hell, I've been doing this for eleven years. I have to be doing something right."

Suddenly, Wilson took up a spoon and made his eyes pop out at it. A minute later, he handed it to me. It was, I had to admit, slightly bent.

"That's pretty good," I said. "But what good does that do America?"

"It's just to prove the point that I possess powers," he said.

"All right, then. Let's get down to brass tacks. What's Boris Yeltsin doing right now?"

Wilson closed his eyes, and I imagined that his head had become a radar dish.

"Ordering a vodka," he said.

"That's plausible," I said.

"Look, here's my background. I give it to all the reporters and fact-checkers. I'm proved in ink."

"I don't want to bother with that," I said, stuffing the packet into my jacket. "I want you to tell me. For instance, how many wars would you say you've prevented?"

"Wars? Well now, I can't say I've prevented any wars, per se. I did prevent an attack at a supermarket once by informing this woman that a psychotic guy who hated women wearing rain scarves was about to come down aisle six for some whipping cream."

"All right, in 1986 you were credited with correctly identifying lies the Russian government had told the US—so how come you can't predict winning lottery numbers?"

"Numbers are only symbols for things. I can only read people or the things themselves."

"But numbers are patternable—there are systems devoted to them. They have defined outcomes, and exist."

"Anyway, I can't. I'm not sure why. Do you think I like working for the government?"

"It doesn't look so bad," I said, nodding to the space-age bachelor pad, "but your poster has to get out of the '70s."

"Hey man, don't go there. Don't mess with my Farrah. Look!"

Wilson pulled out a bed drawer and laid a bulging scrapbook in my lap. It was his collection of thirty magazine covers from 1978, all with Farrah on the cover.

"Are you in counseling?" I asked.

Wilson grabbed the scrapbook back and folded his arms defiantly.

"Can you predict your own actions?" I asked him.

"Not with any accuracy."

"OK, here's one. Back in 1979, you predicted the emergence of the Rubik's Cube. How did that come about?"

"I'm not sure, exactly. I kept dreaming of people turning colored blocks over in their hands."

"Well, is there anything you can do right now, besides magic spoon-bending tricks?"

"It's not magic!" Wilson roared.

"All right. Well, I'm running out of questions."

"You haven't asked me why I don't get a real job."

"Ah, yes," I said.

"You're thinking about how you wish you had your own nice, cushy government office."

"Uh, yeah," I said, bewildered.

"And you're wondering where you can get your own Farrah poster."

"Yes," I said, now flabbergasted. "Where?"

"You can have mine. I've got ten of them." Wilson went into a closet and gave me a rolled-up copy of the Dentyne-smile, red-bathing-suit classic.

"Hell, I guess you're legit," I said. He'd definitely read me correctly.

"Yeah, that's right, man. I'm sick of you dopes razzing me about my authenticity."

"Well, I'm sorry about that," I said. "But as a reporter for the true American public, I have to remain somewhat skeptical."

"That's all right."

"Well, it looks like I got what I came for. Thanks for the 'view,'" I said. I stood up.

"Anytime."

I moved toward the door and stuck out my hand.

"Don't predict anything you don't want to know," I said.

"Don't write anything you wouldn't want to read."

I winced and walked out. This time, I opted to go around the standing line. I went out to the parking lot and stepped right in front of a student driver. I was knocked out of my sandals, but didn't sustain any serious damage. I stuck a cigarette in my mouth and cursed. The bastard had to have known it was coming.

Johnny Heart Attack

Death came out of the shadows and sat on the edge of my bed.

"It's time," he said.

"What?"

I was still groggy. I had just woken up from a nightmare. I sensed I was being served bad news.

"It's time. Time to die," the figure said.

Death was wearing a suit and a thin tie. Who knew death would end up looking like Rod Serling? He was smoking, even.

The wild thought occurred to me that Death probably looked different to different people. This was *my* death. Maybe, for some people, death looked like Julia Child or Pavarotti.

"But how?" I complained. "I'm only thirty-four. I'm in bed, for christsakes."

"Heart attack," Death said. "Got you in your sleep. Shoulda quit smoking."

Death flipped his own cigarette out my window.

"Oh, crap!" I said. I was thinking of all the shit I had to get done. I was supposed to go on vacation in a couple of weeks; I was gonna miss that. I wanted to cry, to feel sorry for myself, but I was too curious to know what death was like. Death was tall, dark, and mysterious. Death looked like Rod Serling. Death was dead.

"So, what now?" I said. "Do we go see what life would have been like if I'd never been born, or do we see how people take the news of my death, or are we going straight to hell?"

"Hell," Death said. "That's a laugh." He lit another smoke.

"Well, what?" I said. Now I was fully awake. I was as awake as a dead person could be.

"We're gonna go meet some other dead people," Death said.

"Oh, like in heaven?"

"No," Death said. "At the bowling alley."

"Do I have to get dressed?" I asked.

"I don't know. Do you normally wear clothes when you go out?"

"Right," I said. I started putting on some clothes. When I was finished, I noticed that the clothes magically reappeared back on the hangars. No one was going to notice them missing. It was just like Death to cover his tracks.

When I was ready, I followed Death out of my apartment. I thought about my friends, my girlfriend, how lucky they were to be alive, and cursed internally. They had no idea how good they had it. They had no idea I was dead. I wanted to say goodbye, *something*.

"We can't do that," Death said. "Come on, we're gonna be late."

Once we were outside, I wondered if we were going to hail a cab. More likely, I thought as I considered it, dead people would probably take public transportation.

Neither, as it turned out. Death and I floated up into the sky and flew over streetlamps and houses, breathing in the cool, invigorating night air. Unseen birds chirped merrily in the trees, a sound that reminded me of the sadness of drinking till dawn. We arrived in short order at this bowling alley I'd heard of but had never been to before, the Diversey Rock and Bowl, and landed gently in front of it.

Death opened the door, and I was astonished to see how crowded the place was so early in the morning.

Bon Jovi's "You Give Love A Bad Name" was blasting out of innumerable speakers. Strobe lights flashed and colored light patterns rotated. We walked past a game room where, I noticed, the games didn't have token slots.

"That's the good thing about being dead," Death said. "You're comped everywhere you go."

I stopped in my tracks when I realized Jimi Hendrix was playing a game of Defender.

"Hey! Is that Jimi Hendrix? Hey wait! I gotta talk to him!"

"There'll be time later," Death said. "He's always here. Come on. What size shoe do you wear?"

"Ten and a half," I said.

Death told the man behind the counter my number, and the man gave me a size eleven. I protested this, but Death put a hand on my arm. "Just take them. He knows that ten-and-a-halfs will pinch your toes and affect your game. That's his job."

I took the shoes and put them on, and I felt instant comfort. They were the best-fitting shoes I'd ever worn.

"Now I understand why all the hip kids are stealing these," I said.

"Come on, let's go," Death said. "Let's introduce you to the team."

"Team?"

"Yeah, we're on the Frosty Pints."

I followed Death to a lane in the far corner. Everyone was wearing an identical light-blue knit shirt with his or her name scrawled across the breast pocket. Death handed me a shirt out of a box. I didn't approve of the color, but what are you gonna do? You take what death gives you.

"I'm Rod Cirrhosis, by the way," Death said. "Stop thinking of me as Death. I didn't kill you; your heart did."

"So you *are* Rod Serling!" I said, astonished.

"No, I'm just a Rod Serling impersonator."

"Oh, I didn't know there was much of a demand for those."

"There wasn't. That's why I was a schoolteacher who drank himself to death. Let's introduce you around."

I met Shirley first. Shirley was a red-haired woman in her forties.

"Hiya, honey," she said in a raspy voice, "I'm Shirley Throat Cancer."

Next I met Bob. Bob looked like an overstuffed sofa. He shook my hand. "Bob Heart Attack," he said and did a ridiculous pantomime, à la Fred Sanford, of a man having "The Big One." He chuckled jovially.

"Why are they telling me how they died?" I asked Rod.

"It's common courtesy when you meet people."

"Oh."

So that's how I started out in death: introducing myself as Johnny Heart Attack.

Kevin Ski Accident. Sue Broken Back. Phil Suicide. Wendy Malpractice. Henry Gunshot.

This group, along with Rod, Shirley and Bob, was my bowling team.

Tonight the rival team was composed of dead Chicago TV newscasters and newsmen: Fahey Flynn, Phil Walters, Floyd Kalber, Gene Siskel, Tim Weigel. "Why does your team only have five members?" I asked Walters.

"Oh, we're saving spots for Harry Volkman and Harry Porterfield. We're expecting them any day now."

Ten frames later, the Cast-Aways were high-fiving each other and sleeving their bowling balls. I'd bowled the best game of my death, but it still wasn't good enough. Flynn picked up an impossible Baby Split in the last frame that sealed our fate.

"Don't sweat it, kid," Phil Suicide said. "I used to let stuff like this bother me. We'll get 'em next time, huh?"

Most of our team repaired to the Lucky Strike Lounge to drown our sorrows. The Budweiser was free, as were the Slim Jims, beer nuts, pork rinds, and anything else we wanted.

"Eat up and enjoy!" Bob said. "It's not like another heart attack's gonna hurt either of us!" He laughed uproariously.

I smiled and found my hands tapping on the bar involuntarily to Def Leppard's "Pyromania."

Rod's attentions, for a while, were focused on a pretty woman in red, who was hovering about, looking seductive. When she finally drifted off, Rod came back over.

"Hey," I said. "I was wondering about something. Um, where do I, uh, live?"

Rod turned his back to me and announced loudly to our team, "Hey everybody! He said it!" The Frosty Pints all raised their glasses in unison and toasted me, laughing.

"You mean," Rod said, "Where do you 'reside'?"

"Uh, yeah," I said, my face reddening with embarrassment. Being dead somehow hadn't affected that.

"You'll start out with an apartment on the top level of my garage. You know, like Fonzie."

"Oh, OK."

"It's a nice place," Rod said. "You'll like it. Best part is, the rent is never due."

Suddenly the whole lounge jerked away, and Rod and I were flying again. This time, we were in a weird hovercraft-thing that zoomed over the tops of trees at tremendous speeds.

"Where are we going?" I asked over the whine of the engine.

Rod told me he was taking me for my enlightenment. I wasn't officially dead until I'd received ultimate knowledge. The Theory of Everything was about to be revealed.

The hovercraft landed in front of a giant castle in the Scottish countryside. I was ushered in through a large entranceway and brought to a medieval-looking basement that was empty, except for a wooden chair and a metal helmet that was hanging above it from a rafter.

Rod stood on the side, watching the proceedings. I was now in the care of John Entwhistle, the dead bassist for The Who.

"Hi," he said. "I'm John Coke Overdose."

He motioned for me to sit in the chair and slowly pulled down the helmet. Rod started phasing in and out, turning from a solid mass to TV snow, as he smiled in that tight, squinty way the real Rod Serling had smiled.

"This is gonna hurt a little," Entwhistle said.

The buzzing noise made me leap. Cold sweat ran down my back, and my heart hammered in my chest. I was back in my bedroom. I felt my arms. I was flesh. I wasn't dead. John Entwhistle was gone. Rod Serling Impersonator Man was no where to be found.

As I caught my breath, my alarm clock continued to howl. When I finally got my head together, I ripped the cord out of the wall, silencing it.

I threw the Mind of God out the window.

It was time to quit smoking, I decided.

Bullets Have
No Effect

The government can't kill me. At first this was a purely bureaucratic problem—appeals, paperwork and general ineptness. Now, ten years of incarceration later, to the prosecutor's dismay, this has become a *physical* problem.

In the state of Texas, lethal injection is the way they kill death row inmates, guilty or, often enough, not guilty. They place you on a gurney, strap you down, and give you an opportunity to say a few words. (I always say, "Hello.") Then, at the warden's signal, a curtain is raised so the witnesses can see. A few solutions are released into the IV drips; one is potassium chloride, which is intended to stop the heart. This is the part of the show where the inmate is supposed to die so that the crowd can go home satisfied.

The problem with this method is that it fails to work. At least, it has failed to work three times so far. Dismayed, enraged, embarrassed, exhausted, the screws finally gave up, stating that there must be something wrong with the chemicals being administered. For sure, heads were going to roll for this one, the death administrators said. The same chemicals that were pumping around in my veins did not fail to kill, however, a mouse that was summoned as a stand-in. The mouse dropped dead on cue. I only felt slightly tingly.

The following day could have been a reenactment of the first: same people, same time, same room. Only this time, it was a new batch of chemicals.

One, two, three.

Nothing.

One, two, three.

Nothing.

People started to get fidgety. They thought a fix was in. Maybe one of the executioners was behind this. Maybe I'd promised somebody money. People swore I would die. The story was all over the headlines. The tabloids thought I was Rasputin. They thought I was evil incarnate.

It got so that I was eventually shipped to a new facility, with new executioners and new chemicals. They said they'd given me enough potassium chloride to kill five hundred men.

Hello. Hello. Hello.

I was getting to be quite a problem for the state of Texas. I was a regular thorn in the side of the governor, William H. Nance. They said I'd killed a little girl by strangulation. I was described as a loner, a freak, a monster. I needed to be abolished. I needed to be extinguished. Authorities went to Plan B.

They went to Zyklon B.

I breathed in hydrogen cyanide as if it were a rose-scented breeze.

The governor was sweating on TV. Reporters mobbed him. His council was under fire. If they could not put down a child-killer, what kind of administration was this? My photo was in the papers. I was the poster boy for every underdog politician who had dreams of office. The foundations were crumbling. If I wasn't covered with dirt soon, the Socialists could take over. It was getting that bad.

Electrocution just gave me indigestion.

They managed to overturn some laws and brought back hanging just for me. How sweet. I hung. I hung around so long it made people sick. I made choking noises, but mostly for effect. No one likes to see a hanging man hung improperly. I think that's because it makes people think of brain damage. No one likes to think about brain damage.

Around then, I noticed that my food rations were getting smaller. They "forgot" water. I understood that they meant to weaken me, if not kill me outright, by starvation. This was all behind the scenes. I told my lawyer about this and he sent up a squeal that was heard all the way to D.C.

Now we've got some attention. I am called Houdini, a vampire, a mutant, the devil.

The governor has met with the president, who has decided somehow that it's allowable for me to be killed by a firing squad. Hell, the president, he does what he wants.

My lawyer yells "cruel and unusual" until he's blue in the face, but no one listens.

"He was not meant to die," he says. "God is willing it. He is an innocent man."

I am bound to a chair and hooded. Twenty meters away, five shooters aim at my heart.

Bullets have no effect.

The media loves the story. There's enough fish food here to nibble on for a century. Two centuries.

I am submerged underwater for three hours. I come out as if I've just woken up from a nap. I feel rather good. I don't even have pruning.

There are attempted decapitations, surprise assaults with samurai swords, but they fail. Death runs off me.

Finally, Washington decides that this is enough. My execution is stayed, just to clear my smiling face from the headlines. I am a bogeyman to some, a hero to others. Some guy in California has started a church around me. Nineteen percent of the American people say they would consider joining it.

I am moved to a secret location. Slowly, I drop out of the papers.

Time goes by; sweet time. I read books, I answer letters, I start painting, all from my little jail cell. Then, one day, I have a visitor. His name is Harry. Harry smells like Old Spice. His haircut is bad; his suit is worse. Harry comes into a meeting room with me and tells me I'm entitled to representation.

My lawyer is on vacation in the Bahamas. I think they know that, but even if he wasn't away, I wouldn't have summoned him. The poor guy needs a break from all this. I welcome the opportunity to meet, and I say so.

We meet in a mostly empty yellow room with only one window up high covered in chicken coop wire. Security at the doors. Me and Harry across a table from one another. No cuffs, just leg irons.

"I'm from a place the American public doesn't know about," Harry says.

"That must be nice," I say.

Harry grimaces and gets serious. He tells me that he is from a place the government has nicknamed "Perfect Executions."

"Quite simply," Harry says. "We kill people. Mostly, we kill people in other countries who get in our way. We're a tool in the box of Democracy. Quite often we're the knife in the back of a warlord. We're a car bomb waiting for a dignitary. We're poison in the cup of a conglomerate head that doesn't play ball."

"What does this have to do with me?" I ask.

Harry looks at me like I'm the dumbest guy on earth.

"I'm going to kill you," Harry says.

"So it does have a lot to do with me."

Harry's idea (and I have to admit, it's a good one) is to blow me up. They're going to arrange for me to be on a yard walk at the prison, and a nearby military base is going to "accidentally" fire a missile and blow me to smithereens. Harry is candid about how the other prisoners will not be in the yard at the time and how he's going to laugh like hell when I'm a pile of stinking guts.

"Going to tell me when, or are you going to let it be a surprise?" I say.

"I'll surprise you, how about that?"

"I like surprises," I say.

I could have told my lawyer, Bernie, all this, but I decide not to. Maybe Bernie likes surprises too. Days pass; then weeks; then two months. Then, one day, I'm out in the yard while the rest of the prison is under lockdown. I feel like I'm being watched carefully through gun sights.

It looks like this is the day.

Way out in the distance, I see something black. It's just a dot, but this dot whistles. It hums and vibrates. I can feel its velocity almost before I can make it out.

I look at the gun tower, at the old coots up there with their high-powered rifles and their death lust, and I smile and turn my back.

The explosion is terrific.

It is cataclysmic, deafening, literally Earthshaking. A good quarter of the prison is destroyed by the errant warhead. The gun towers collapse. The fences are blown down. The grass is on fire.

The papers will later reveal that 150 prisoners died, fourteen guards, ten visitors, and one photojournalist. "Collateral damage," I think they call that.

I dust myself off and step over a piece of fallen concrete as sirens wail and smoke rises. Like a creature reborn, I make my way back to the land of the living.

Mercurochrome

In the dark of the kitchen, my cigarette glows. Across the room, the Mr. Coffee gurgles. A snapshot of lightning occasionally lights the room.

I can't sleep through storms.

I might stay awake for hours like this, giving in to my insomnia, only to be rewarded by sunlight and a precise headache. But, alternately, I might hear the faint hiss of a driver's error on the expressway that borders our backyard, followed by the guttural scrape and buckle of metal on metal; the harrowing crash of glass; snapping trees and silenced screams.

Tonight is one of those nights. There is a rough bang followed by aluminum can crumple then a deeper, more ominous sound of a muffler gone loose or off from underbrush. A final thump not unlike a fist hitting a pillow, then nothing but drilling rain.

I put down the nail file and wave my cigarette quickly under the tap, switch off the coffee maker, and hurry upstairs to my husband Gary, who is asleep in bed, unaware. When I shake him he wakes instantly, sensing the electric charge in the air. His eyes search mine for confirmation and I nod. We both dress. I pull the medical bag from the closet. Gary gets the lantern.

We move across the saturated lawn as water seeps around our feet. Rain blasts against the reinforced golf umbrella. As soon as we see the headlamps of the battered car, Gary stops and calls 911 on his cell phone.

A woman is lying ten meters from us, face down, not moving. A man is twisted at a cruel angle in the driver's seat, his legs obscured by mangled steel, a cowboy hat still affixed to his head.

We go to the woman first. Her eyes are blue and lifeless. She is beautiful. I can smell her perfume through the downpour. I place a blanket on her; we have lots of blankets.

The man is talkative, animated by fresh shock, but we've seen this before. We're only witnessing the final jerks of life. He laughs as blood pours out of him at a tremendous rate.

"My wife," he gasps. "She OK?"

"She's fine," Gary says. "The ambulance is on its way."

"I thought this was the exit," the man sobs.

Gary shakes his head. "Up ahead," he says.

"I guess I *made* an exit," the man says, attempting a joke.

"It's a common mistake," Gary tells him as he gives the man a drink of water from his canteen.

Above us, through the branches, a trucker shouts from the road.

"I called for help when I saw him go off the highway," he calls to us. "Anything I can do?"

We can hardly hear him through the rain.

"No," Gary and I shout back in unison.

"OK, then," the man calls back; we can hear him only faintly. I wonder whether he's relieved that we won't require him to navigate down the steep, brambled slope—that he doesn't have to see what we see. Then we hear him again:

"Are they gonna make it?"

As if we're doctors; as if we're qualified to say. Our medical bag is full of the most ineffective of medical supplies: Band-Aids, Q-Tips, aspirin, Mercurochrome.

"Everybody's gonna make it, I think," Gary shouts to the trucker, just as the injured driver whispers, "Shit . . ." and expires.

It's strange here in the night without our neighbors, Amber and Dwayne. But the Falks' house stands across the yard, dark, empty, and for sale. It's the only residence besides ours within a half mile of here. The Falks are now in Tucson, where Dwayne is at a new job. I know Amber misses times like this. We talk occasionally. Almost the first thing she will ask when she calls is, "Any turn-outs?" Turn-outs are what we call the people who mistake a pull-off on I-83 for an exit that seems overdue and take a slide down a seventy-five-meter slope into the wild end of our property line.

It's an unsafe place for a pull-off. It's deceptive, especially at night and with the actual exit so close. You have fog or rain or sleet or darkness or distraction, and things happen. Why the highway department has not remedied this hazard is a mystery; surely someone is keeping statistics and knows that this is an accident-prone area. We've met the same ambulance drivers, the same police, and the same tow-truck operators more than once. Gary and I have shuddered at the waste of it all, but our drafted letters have never been mailed. Sometimes we wonder at the capacity of our own ghoulishness: our need for disfigurement, for tragedy; our addiction to it. Our lives so far have been otherwise free of grief and misfortune. Our childhoods were not ripped apart by divorce or molestation; family members have not been afflicted with incurable diseases. Perhaps we fear the inevitable breach of this shelter.

We view horrific gore from our backyard, but once you're beyond the blood, there is calm in knowing death a little better and knowledge in realizing that it does not care what it looks like. Ultimately, there's also relief in knowing that, at least for now, it's not *you*.

Amber and Dwayne understood this. We found them outside one chilly night when a teenage driver turned out into our yard ten years ago. We found Amber and Dwayne in possession of the medical bag I hold now; with the lantern Gary keeps.

That first time, the sight of blood-soaked grass and the smell of dripping oil and burnt flesh made me retch. Only when authorities arrived did I calm down a little. That's when Amber put a hand on my shoulder and said, in a way that was part apology, part warning, and part something else, "This happens a lot."

It's happened eight times in ten years—regularly enough that I know the type of weather that causes it and will become sleepless when that weather arrives. I have a crash log in my desk, entries written in longhand in blue ballpoint pen in a cheap drug store notebook. In it, I list names and ages (when I know them), makes and models of vehicles, personal traits of the victims, injuries sustained, causes of death.

Sometimes I look at the log and wonder about the empty lines that I haven't filled yet. I've caught Gary doing the same. Somewhere, someone living now will be entered on the blanks.

On that night years ago when we all met for the first time, Amber, Dwayne, Gary and I became a team, a united organism. After that, we were not unlike soldiers ordered to the front, emboldened only by each other's company. In numbers, we felt like we could face down anything. We assisted the unfortunate victims however we could, expressing words of comfort, but usually there was little we could do. We rarely had to alert each other. Asleep or not, it was something we were always listening for. When we heard the telltale sounds, we emerged from our homes and walked across the yard, hyperaware, wondering what shape death would or would not take.

—⁑—

When Gary and I learn that someone has bought the Falks' place, we don't talk about it much, except to hope aloud that they will be nice people, hopefully not too young or too old. Hopefully with kids already grown up or decided against.

On the Saturday the movers arrive, we're having coffee and reading the newspaper on our wraparound upper-level porch. The porch was a major selling point of this house for us. When we first saw it, we imagined ourselves just as we are on this particular day, sitting here with our coffee and newspaper, eye-level with the surrounding tree cover.

That would be nice, we said.

The Falks' house has a fully finished basement with a workroom and a built-in Tiki bar. Gary was always envious of that bar, but he would never have traded the porch. Not in a million years.

We give a friendly wave and shout hello when we see the new couple, and they wave back. They seem about our age—early forties. We don't see any kids, and no kids' stuff is being unloaded.

"Let us know if we can help with anything," we say.

To Gary I say, "We'll stop over tonight with cookies or wine."

"They won't want to be bothered," Gary says.

"Believe me," I say, gesturing to the wilderness that surrounds us, "they'll want to be bothered."

We visit that night and meet Rick and Maggie Miller, transplants from New York City. Rick is in the banking software industry, and has taken a job with less plane travel required. Maggie is planning on finding a job teaching ESL to grade-school children. It's confirmed: no kids.

The bottle of wine gets opened amid a hundred boxes that haven't been, yet. I admire Maggie's willingness to let things lie—to admit to herself that she's done enough for one day and relax. I tell her the things I know about her house. Helpful things. Pleasant things.

Gary and Rick talk golf and cars—passions they share.

We invite them over to our place for a tour and then sit on the porch with some open beers. At some point, we notice as they glance toward the expressway, but all Gary says is, "It's a little closer than we'd like, but luckily it never gets too loud. Terri actually finds the traffic soothing."

Many chats and visits later, Gary and Rick have been to the ranges and the local baseball games, while Maggie and I have been antiquing and biking the many trails that wind around here. One day Rick is clearing away old twigs in the backyard and finds pieces of vehicles—reflectors, other odd parts.

"Just stuff flung off from the highway?" he asks Gary.

"Maybe. But some cars have actually turned out too soon," Gary says. "Some cars have been *down* here."

Another month, and then another. Gary is promoted to Vice President at Barlowe Refrigeration. My online-based jewelry business starts to attract more customers. Now we're into winter, the first snow of the year. It's another night when I can't sleep; this time, I'm thinking of the first snow of the year three years ago, when an SUV flipped over and a man named Marty Sikes was crushed.

I read in the quiet of the kitchen and smoke. Outside, the wind swirls; white, innocent. I turn a page in the supermarket novel I'm reading when I hear a noise like a gate at a horse track flinging open. There are heavy thuds and crashes, followed by silence. I can't see anything much out of the window—it's too far back.

Gary is already up and dressing. We get the bag, lantern, and blankets and go outside. The fat flakes whirl around us, landing and melting on our faces. The moon lights up the snow, turning it blue. The Millers' house is dark and still.

This time, it's a woman in a pickup truck. She is unconscious, twisted against the roof of the crumpled cab. Blue jeans, Harley T-shirt, a boozy smell. There's a pack of Parliaments in the snow.

Gary calls 911 while I reach in for a pulse.

From behind, we hear footfalls that startle us, and I wonder if the same sound scared the Falks on that night ten years ago. The Millers look like ghosts. Blank-faced, they stare at the truck, not comprehending.

Then they look at Gary and me, at our medical bag and lantern. At our composure and preparedness.

Something begins to take hold.

I hand a blanket to Maggie; her fingers close on it tightly, automatically.

I lead her to the body.

Ghostlike

The first thing you lose when you die is your motor skills. You become almost weightless and nearly invisible, which is nice, but it's hell trying to get anywhere.

I spent my first day as a ghost trapped in the video arcade of the North Park Mall. I was stuck between a game called *Zombleed*, which involved sawing zombies in half with a chainsaw, and another, intended for girls, called *Pinky the Unicorn*. No matter how I struggled, I couldn't move out of the space in which I'd found myself.

The players' absorption in their respective games kept them from noticing me, but I soon attracted the attention of the two Indian gentlemen who ran the arcade. I saw them discussing something. They were both wearing bright orange vests with name tags. Sanjee pointed in my direction and the other, Muhammad, squinted across the room. Muhammad was just going on shift.

I thought of them as brothers, although I'm not sure whether they actually were. Their rich, black hair was stacked high on their heads and it seemed that they had similar features, but maybe this was just my imagination. They were very calm; I admired that. They came up and looked above and around me, looking for the source of me. They put their hands through me, and then concluded that some sort of magnetism between the two machines was probably responsible for the pillar of bending waves that distorted the air . . . They moved one game away from the wall.

That was all it took. I sprang loose.

I was momentarily exhilarated. I drifted like a balloon until I bumped up between a column and a planter close to Mariella's Pretzel Shack and got stuck again. During my confinement at this new location, I observed the business closely. Mariella was a short Italian woman in her late thirties. She kept her long brown hair pinned under a white cap. Mariella struck me as hardworking—maybe too hardworking. She had a sign posted advertising for help.

Mariella looked at me curiously a few times and even walked through me once to see what the deal was. She seemed to think I was a problem with the light, because she directed some of the mall's physical-plant personnel to the lights above her little shack. The men checked them out and then told her that the lights were working fine; they would not be replaced until they needed replacing.

Mariella studied me, and I studied her. Since I was unsure of my role as a newborn apparition, I hoped maybe I'd learn something from observation. I gathered from the conversations Mariella had with her customers that she was divorced and had a daughter named Rosemary who was in college. Her most frequent customer was this one guy who wore a red jogging suit, though he didn't appear to be at all athletic.

Jimbo, this man called himself. Jimbo hit on Mariella as if she were the most sought-after princess in the land. Maybe to his eyes Mariella was a princess, or maybe her circumstances had reduced her to being attainable to the likes of Jimbo—at least in his estimation. Who could say? I'd never before observed someone eat his weight in mustard-covered hot pretzels.

One day, despairing of something interesting to talk about, Mariella pointed to me and asked Jimbo what he thought. Did I look odd to him at all? Did the light almost look like a body? Walk through it, she urged; it's cold. It's the weirdest thing.

Jimbo couldn't, or didn't want to, see me. He walked through me, flapping his long arms and going, "What? What? See? Nothing!" This may have cost him any chance he had with Mariella.

"You ever take a vacation?" Jimbo asked Mariella. "You work too much. You need to go on a vacation. You should come fishing with me sometime."

"Huh!" Mariella snorted. "You think I can leave this place in the hands of these kids I got working for me? I'd have the health department shut me down in a week! If they showed up for work at all, that is. They're always quitting on me."

As I watched Mariella's activities and the goings-on in the pretzel shack, I continued to struggle to gain mobility. I enjoyed watching things from my little corner, but I had a nagging sense that I had to get somewhere and, not only that, that I had to *do* something. Wasn't it the nature of ghosts to be restless? Well, then, I was restless.

—◦◦◦—

I'd died in the most ridiculous of ways. A power line fell ahead of the bus I was on. The front of the bus exploded in a fireball, and there was a lot of smoke and screaming; sparks were spitting all over the place. There was this vibration of uncontained power in the ground. The line sputtered. It hummed. It hissed. Some people panicked and tried to get off the bus; I was one of them. It was on fire. I touched a metal railing and that was it: my last action. I was thirty-one.

Now I was dead. I supposed, anyway. Having not received any kind of universal knowledge or guide to the afterlife, I wasn't quite sure what was happening, but I knew this much: I was ghostlike. I wanted to move, and I needed to do something.

After a few days, it got so that I could make slight, jerky motions that would carry me an inch or two. Slowly, I inched away from the pretzel shack and positioned myself in the foot traffic that was passing by Rothbart's Jewelry store. Eventually, I maneuvered to the northwest corner of the first floor, which terminated at a vitamin store, and gradually began to have more control over my movements. By day five, I was floating a good three inches off the polished tiles and could move about pretty much at will, like a proper ghost and had even regained use of my hands and arms. Though I seemed to have access to any area of the mall, when I attempted to leave the premises, a force at the exits repelled me.

By my seventh day, I could easily have ascended to the second floor using the escalator, but my lofty goal was to levitate myself there with my own ghostly power. Why did I need to get to the second floor? I knew this much, now, too: someone named Colin was up there. For some reason, I had to meet Colin.

Using all of my energy, I concentrated on levitating. Up I went, just like a real ghost, and landed safely on the second floor near Carson's department store, where a sullen-looking sixteen-year-old boy sat on a bench, watching a row of TVs.

Colin looked like he could have been the lead in a movie about troubled teens. He wore a faded denim jacket that reeked of cigarettes. His long brown hair hung over his old-soul eyes. His jeans were torn at the knees. His gym shoes had been drawn on with a ballpoint pen: anarchy symbols, bands I'd never heard of.

I knew, without being told, that Colin had a broken home and that my mission was to try to improve his life if I could. Why was this my mission? I had no idea. Maybe, before you pass on completely, some final deed is required of you.

Colin was sitting on a bench—it was more of a slab, really—watching the row of TVs and ignoring the biology homework that he'd brought along. Colin wasn't making much progress on the homework. The book was closed, and he was watching a rap artist sing about his bling and his thing.

Colin watched the rappers, and the rappers that followed them, and then the glamorous teen idols that followed them. At some point, Colin opened his biology workbook and attempted a few questions, but this was soon put aside. When the mall was closing, he left his homework assignment on the bench.

I secreted the page away and looked it over. Though I'd always been horrible at science and math, I could tell from Colin's answers that he could not be doing well in this class. I resolved to help. I traversed the mall that night until I hit upon an idea.

The next afternoon, when Colin appeared on the bench, I placed a note near him.

LOCKER 508

FIND KEY BENEATH THE BENCH

WHAT'S INSIDE IS YOURS

— MAGIC BOX

Colin read the note and looked around suspiciously. There wasn't anyone standing close to him, except for an old couple looking at sunglasses in Sunglass Hut and a woman perusing sweaters near the entrance of Carson's. Colin looked up, but there was no third floor.

He stuffed the note in his pocket and looked beneath the bench. Then he took the key and started walking slowly, his eyes darting furtively beneath the protection of his bangs. He didn't walk to the lockers immediately. He made a loop of the second floor first, probably to see if he was being followed. Once he was confident that he wasn't, he turned down the hallway where the lockers were.

Colin arrived at locker 508 and glanced around. There were only a few people coming into the mall from the outside doors, but no one else was around. He inserted the key and removed an item that I had placed inside the night before, a book called *Biology the Easy Way*.

He opened the cover and flipped through the book. My heart swelled at the thought of this good thing I'd done. Now, Colin would know that someone cared about his well-being and education, even if his parents didn't. I imagined this little act having a ripple effect on his entire life. He would never forget the mysterious stranger who had helped him out, who had led him to embrace the sciences and become a respected biologist.

I followed Colin on his way back to the mall concourse. Then I had all the wind knocked out of me when I saw him deposit the book in the garbage can and leave the mall.

Maybe it had been presumptuous of me to assume that such a trifling deed would change Colin's life and allow the gates of the afterlife to swing wide, but I was thoroughly crushed, crushed as only a heartless teenager can crush someone.

The next day Colin came back to his usual spot by the TV sets. Again, he neglected his homework almost exclusively for the endless stream of video imagery. Today his posture seemed hostile, like he was defiantly waiting for some adult to show up and inquire about how he'd liked the gift. He seemed prepared to tell this person to fuck the hell off.

As he waited for this encounter, Colin tore open several sugar packets and poured the contents into his mouth. I wondered, horrified, whether this was his dinner.

No wonder his schoolwork was suffering. How could he be expected to concentrate without a decent meal in his stomach? Inspired by this realization, I absconded to Portillo's Hot Dogs and inserted myself into the assembly line, where the employees were throwing together sandwiches for hungry customers at their usual incredible speed. My theft of two red hots was not noticed amid the gyrations of the workers. I delivered the hot dogs to the locker.

Relieved to find Colin still at his post, I dropped a new note nearby.

EAT AT JOE'S

SEE MAGIC BOX

Colin read the note and stood up hastily, looking every which way for the creep stalker, but no one was close. He went to the locker and opened it up. He might have been concerned about some psycho poisoning him, but if he was actually hungry, I doubted he would be able to resist the tempting smells wafting directly into his face. My assumption was correct; he ate both hot dogs without hesitation. After looking around to confirm that no one was going to approach him, he headed for the parking lot.

I smiled at this small success. Eager to continue to make an inroad to him, that evening I removed a pair of gym shoes from Maury's Shoes that looked about his size and placed them the locker. Colin's shoes were in bad repair, so I figured he'd appreciate the gesture. The next day, Colin came to the bench and found a note I'd left for him.

JUST DO IT

— MAGIC BOX

Colin opened the locker, examined the shoes, then placed them back inside. He took out a note card, wrote something and placed it in the locker as well. This started a note exchange that lasted over the course of a few days.

Colin: I DON'T WANT YOUR SHOES.

Magic Box: SORRY. WHAT DO YOU WANT?

Colin: MONEY.

Magic Box: I CAN'T GIVE YOU MONEY. WHAT ELSE DO YOU WANT?

Colin: MONEY.

Magic Box: I CAN ONLY GIVE YOU SOMETHING SUBSTANTIAL.

Colin: MONEY IS SUBSTANTIAL. GIVE ME A HUNDRED DOLLARS.

Magic Box: HOW ABOUT A PART-TIME JOB?

Colin: WHAT JOB?

Magic Box: PRETZEL SHACK. GOOD JOB. FRIENDLY BOSS. BUT DON'T BOTHER UNLESS YOU'LL BE ON TIME AND WORK HARD.

When he received my last note about the job opening, Colin seemed confident that he had uncovered the mystery of who was sending him the notes. He passed by the shack several times, looking at Mariella, trying to see whether she would take any notice of him. Finally, he approached the shack and purchased a pretzel. He kept staring at Mariella even after the transaction was complete.

"The mustard's over there," she said

"Um, OK, thanks," Colin said. He hesitated.

"Need something else?"

"Uh, no." Colin turned away but came back after a couple of steps. "Hey, you're looking for someone?" He nodded at the "HELP WANTED" sign.

"Yes, we are. Do you want to fill out an application?"

"Yeah. Thanks."

Mariella handed the form to Colin. "Here you are."

"Thanks."

Colin wandered off, looking more confused than ever. If Mariella was the stranger behind the magic box, she hadn't acted like it. Laughing to myself, I went back to the video arcade to create more optical distortions.

When I floated past the pretzel shack a few days later, I was gratified to find that Mariella had given Colin a chance. He was behind the counter, head bent in concentration as he rolled out dough in long sheets. Mariella was standing behind him, gently coaching. In the same omniscient way I'd known I had to do something for Colin, I knew that this job was an important step for him. Mariella was going to teach him something and make him feel good about himself—something he hadn't felt in a long time. And I knew something else as well: while his road was just beginning, mine was finally ending.

I found myself ahead of a janitor's broom, being pushed towards the north exit, my motor skills depleted again. The janitor kept pushing in his erratic manner until we were at the doors of the mall. Before, whenever I'd come close to these doors, I would bump against an invisible barrier that was similar to the feeling of two magnets opposing each other. I hadn't been able to get through, no matter how hard I'd tried.

But now this barrier had vanished. I stood at the exit, facing the light, terrified but hopeful.

I summoned the nerve to walk forward on heavy, human legs, and passed into whatever came next.

Orbit

A pparently my father is a New Age guru. I found this out yesterday while I was watching TV. A commercial came on late at night and I saw my dad touting a miracle book that solves everything.

Did you ever wonder who those people are with the wet, plastic smiles on your TV set, pitching a folding exercise machine or turnip slicer? Those people are someone's sons and daughters. Those people are someone's mothers and fathers. Those people had families at one time, before they left orbit.

In the commercial, my dad looked older, balder, more insane. His eyes glittered with some kind of sparkle that usually seems forbidden to most of us workaday stiffs. The woman beside him (is he fucking her?) was the same way. Her hair was this raft of sprayed-up blonde hair, her smile was a thousand watts, and her eyes were oceanic. Nobody home.

I was fairly crocked when this scene presented itself to me in color and sound. I was smoking my lungs out and drinking cold Heinekens with my friend Abe. We weren't even looking for shows to watch. We wanted to watch commercials. Commercials have become the point. When we watch them, we feel superior to all of America. We alone see America for the corrupt, bloated, greedy pig that it is, and here is the parade in front of our bleary eyeballs—attorneys, car-wrecking companies, air fresheners, all forms of miracle products, pompadoured evangelists, wild-eyed game show hosts, and screaming Japanese.

On the work table behind us were sheaves of cartoon drafts done in Sharpie pen. We do an occasional cartoon called *Barn Destroyer,* which is published irregularly in alternative magazines that sometimes remember to send a check. Our method is this: I draw whatever comes into my head, a one-panel, and Abe writes something insane beneath it. Sometimes the drawing is good, sometimes not. Sometimes the writing is good, sometimes not. This method gives us one cartoon in ten that's worth publishing.

But, that day, the cartoon frenzy was over. We had worked for an hour or so, but then we'd become bored. It was more fun to impress each other with our genius, drink beer, smoke, listen to Public Enemy, and of course, watch the glistening orb: the mighty chrome TV, which informs as well as crushes our fragile American souls.

The Gulf War was on. Our forces were clashing in the desert. There were playing cards to prove it. It was entertainment for some; however, it was not entertainment for us. Abe and I talked about the (remote) possibility of a draft.

"I'm not going," he said. "I'm 4-F."

"Why are you 4-F?" I said.

Abe pointed to his Converse-clad peds. "I have flat feet."

I'm not so lucky. My feet are curved and I'm not clinically insane. George Bush, Sr. would feed me right into the cannon.

"Well, I'm not going either," I said. "I'll go to Amsterdam. Fuck that."

And so on. Abe and I like to talk. We like to talk like talking is going to change America. Like we're going to pull some kind of Yippie stunt that will wake everybody up to what a lie this country is. Etc.

Our brains and egos are the size of jetliners. We know everything there is to know. We see our faces being chiseled in the Cartoon Hall of Fame.

—◦◦◦—

Abe's father is missing. My father is in Hawaii. Both skipped out on our families when we were young. Abe and I have a lot in common.

I haven't heard from my father in over six years. The last word from him was a birthday card on my sixteenth birthday. No money, just a note to wish me a happy birthday and some joke about not being a menace to society when I got my driver's license.

OK. Animosity. Deep feelings of hatred toward the absent father. You got it. That's me. That's Abe. I have no idea what my dad's been doing—I've just heard some vague rumors of risky business ventures of one sort or another. My mom has kept us kids pretty much in the dark.

Before he took off for parts unknown, Abe's dad was some kind of crazy addict or something. I saw a picture of him once. He looked like that guy who sings for Whitesnake: a total fucking hippie.

So when my dad came on the TV, there was a moment when I was trying to get my brain around how I knew this guy. How many middle-aged guys do I know? It was weird. It took a couple seconds and then, when it hit, I screamed at the TV and pointed.

"What the fuck!? Oh my God!"

"What?! What?!" Abe said.

"That's my fucking *dad*!" I said.

My dad was holding a book called *The Shamanic Wisdom: The Art of Creative Healing*. He was telling me how this book would change my life. The blonde woman was nodding. (Does she blow him?)

It's times like these when I think I can actually feel the Earth move off its axis. Is everything I know a lie?

Like, when I was a kid, I used to think that gas station attendants (back when they used to fill up your tank) were actually spies who were injecting an explosive (technically, they were) into your car, which would detonate about five miles away from the gas station (never happened).

I used to think maybe my Mom was a robot. What happened to my real mom?

I used to think that maybe if you peeled back the glowing part of the moon you'd expose a wood backing, a cheap stage prop. This is what I'm talking about.

My father is not my father.

It took a while for me to settle down.

I wanted to cry. I wanted to heave a brick through the TV. I wanted to puke.

"It's fucking disgusting!" I spit, my stomach aching.

Abe was more philosophical. He is Zen. He is always calm, no matter what.

"He's part of the network," he said. "He's part of the machine. Let it go."

"Do you realize?" I said. "Do you realize that I have a definite problem here? I have to decide whether to read this book or not. I mean, if your father told you a particular book would make you happy, would solve everything, wouldn't you have to read it? What if it *does* solve everything?"

"I wouldn't do it," Abe advised. "Too dangerous. In your state of mind, you could bend. It could force you over to the dark side."

"Oh, hell with that!" I said. "I have good critical thinking skills. I won't be swayed."

"Don't drink the Kool-Aid man, don't drink the Kool-Aid. I'm tellin' ya."

I remember all of this now, a day later, lying in my bedroom/recovery unit. I feel like a human husk, one thrashed and left lying in a dry heap on the summer pavement. My father's pixelated face hangs over me like an ugly wind chime.

I consider that maybe Abe is right. I am too vulnerable to read a book wherein the mysteries of the universe are explained and sanctioned by my own blood, What if I ended up believing his lies again, only this time writ large for the masses?

I think I'll just let the book with the answers sit on the shelf or in the warehouse or wherever they keep books that solve everything.

I'll let my dad be the father to someone else.

Operators are standing by.

Things To Do

My Retreat Buddy's name is Bob. He has worked for In-foDyne for eleven years. I never met Bob before coming to Lake Humpal. I've never, to my knowledge, seen him until this trip, even though he works two floors down in Purchasing.

On Day One, Lew Grinstead, the Captain Stubing of this ridiculousness, had all fifty of us pair off by random number selection. I would have preferred to get my real buddy, Alex. Instead, I got Bob.

Buddies on this retreat do exercises together.

They support each other.

Buddies room together.

Our room is in a lodge called Whispering Pines. The walls in the lobby are glazed logs. Over the fireplace hangs a painting of the founder of StaySweet Industries, R. L. McNaughton. R. L. is bald with black horn-rims. His smile is more of a clench.

Inside Room 509 there are corporate inspiration photographs. Our central photograph, hanging roughly where the TV should be, is a picture of a snow-capped purple mountain. Below it, a caption reads, simply, "Aspire."

There are no phones here. No TV sets. No laptops.

Instead, there are To-Do Lists with StaySweet Industries' logo on them. StaySweet is Lew Grinstead's company. His company is trying to teach our company a thing or two.

I've come to realize that Bob doesn't have much in the way of a personality. If it weren't for the fact that Bob is a rabid Bears fan like myself, I don't think we'd have anything in common.

It's the end of Day One, a day of bombardment. I haven't had one independent thought. It was too much. I'm on my bed, trying to read. Bob wants to talk.

Bob is a company man.

Bob is a family man.

I can tell Bob wishes that I had a family.

Everything for Bob is family.

"Ever come close?" Bob says.

"To what?" I say.

"To marriage."

We've spent the day, almost all of it, under the tutelage of Grinstead's sidekick, Madeleine Scoville, a colorless minion of StaySweet Industries. Today we spent three hours in a conference room called "The Narrative Room," where we shared our stories of identity and purpose.

I'm really tired of sharing.

"Not really, Bob," I say.

Bob is disappointed. He wants desperately for me to have what he has—a comfortable life in the suburbs. He can't believe that I choose to live in the city.

"Don't you get tired of all the garbage blowing around?" Bob says.

"It's a fairly clean city these days," I say, aching to return to my book.

"How about that seminar today?" Bob says.

Since he doesn't specify *which* seminar, I have to ask; otherwise, I'm rude. This is how passive-aggressives have conversations—they force them on others.

"Which one?" I say.

"The one on flowcharting your destiny."

"Oh, yeah, sure. That was great."

I light a cigarette, because I know it will drive Bob nuts. Maybe he'll leave.

As soon as I light up, Bob dives for the air conditioner and plants his face next to the vents. He watches in horror as the blue/grey smoke wafts around the room. He pretends to study a packet nearby. The room is full of packets. It's white with packets. Packets the size of those shingles that line the bottom of the Space Shuttle. Packets called "Inventing Desire." Packets called "The Importance of Brand."

After I finish the smoke, Bob flaps the bathroom door a bit and announces that he's going to bed. "Good night, Bob," I say, turning the page.

Things to Do:

Suffocate Bob with pillow.

On Day Two of the retreat, every department is given "Focus Tasks." Madeleine Scoville tells us these are "back-burner" tasks. We're not expected to work on them openly; rather, we should let them simmer and ripen.

I work in marketing. One of my tasks is to promote MATHO-SAUR, a toy dinosaur that teaches math. As I roam, I am thinking of ways to unleash MATHOSAUR on the populace.

Being outdoors is nice, but unfortunately it's tainted with team-building activities, processes, and matrices. Grinstead is a black-eyed puppet. Scoville is a blonde-haired vampire. Together, they are the tag team of self-immolation, conspiring to suck individuality out of every blood-filled being.

As I participate in these exercises, I occasionally sneak glances at my coworkers and wonder if any of them are in as much pain as I am. Even my friend Alex seems to have swallowed the hook, even though he's made a good living mastering the manipulation of others.

I have drunk beers until dawn with Alex. We have traded sordid college tales. I can't believe he's buying into this stuff. Still, for low-level brainwashing, StaySweet knows how to do it right. In the tradition of other mind programmers, they don't allow you any time alone—time to get perspective and see what a load of shit they're handing you. They get everyone excited and make it socially unacceptable not to be "part of the team."

At various points I have fantasies of strangling our CEO, Newt Holler, the one who's responsible for this. Holler is not at Lake Humpal; he's miles away, probably safely tucked away in a Michigan Avenue penthouse, doing blow off the chest of some high-priced hooker. Meanwhile, I sit on a stump with a crude tribal instrument, getting my head beaten like a drum by a business cult.

Things to Do:

Hang self with bathrobe belt.

That night, it's me and Bob again.

Bob is so into the program, it freaks me out. Today we had a lecture called "Defining Moment." We were told that we all wound up here together for a reason, and that we can trace who we are today (and where we are) to this defining moment. We were asked to think about this, and to be prepared to tell everyone about our defining moment tomorrow.

"So," Bob says, "Got yours?"

I'm on page forty-three in my book. No one knows this, but my novel is the only thing keeping me sane right now.

"Got what?" I say.

"Your moment," Bob says. "Do you know what it is?"

When I first heard this concept of a defining moment, I thought immediately about Jim Morrison. His defining moment, from what I've read about him, was when he was a kid vacationing with his family in the New Mexico desert and they saw a car accident—all these Indians scattered on dawn's highway. Morrison said that one of the souls of the suffering, bleeding Indians leaped into his body. A terrific defining moment. But who had shit like that?

I thought for a while, and I said, "Bob, I'm still waiting for my dead Indian."

God knows what he made of that.

On Day Three, we start with coffee and donuts and then hear a starry-eyed guest speaker named Clive Crump talk for an hour about overcoming obstacles. His words wield some kind of strange methamphetamine power. Everyone around me is ramrod straight in his or her chair, even Alex.

When it's close to noon we're told to get with our Buddies, because we are going to journey to the inner sanctum. At the doorway we pick up small Subway sandwiches and water bottles and put them into our backpacks, and we follow Lew and Madeleine to the Petrified Forest.

The "Petrified Forest" is a bunch of petrified stumps, none of them more than two meters high. They are not majestic. They are not towering. We are supposed to find them inspirational. Bob is agog. He rubs the rock/trees and says, "Wow, imagine how tall this used to be!"

After traipsing through the rocks for an hour, we finally stop to unpack our lunches and I manage to separate myself from Bob. I sidle over to Alex and whisper around my sandwich.

"Jesus," I say. "I've got to get out of here. This shit is driving me nuts."

Alex nods slightly, but he's cautious about it. Clearly, he's not interested in this kind of talk—not here, anyway.

Zip it, his eyes say.

Go with the flow, his eyes say.

Don't rock the boat.

I try a different tack.

"Game day tomorrow. Packers–Bears," I say. "Hate to miss that."

But Alex isn't going there. He has recently had his first child and moved into a larger house. There are stakes. He pretends to read a packet called "Learning to Listen." I get the picture. Eventually, I move away.

I move under a tree to be alone. Inside, I'm quivering. I'm on the cusp of something. When Bob shows up, I tell him I'm leaving.

"What?"

"I'm going, Bob," I say.

I can tell Bob thinks this is UNWELCOME ACTION. This is UNSCRIPTED.

He blinks a few times, trying to compute this.

"It's the last day tomorrow, anyway," I say. "No one will care."

But of course *someone* will care. Our bosses; somebody.

But I can't take another minute. If I have to look at the bland plastic faces of Grinstead and Scoville another second, if I have to hear another word like "brainstorm" or "matrix," I am going to kill someone.

I stand up and pat Bob on the shoulder and toss my packet to the dirt. I push some branches aside.

Bob comes up behind me. "Where are you going?" he says. His Buddy is going AWOL. This is UNTEAMLIKE.

"It's Sunday tomorrow," I say. "Packers–Bears. I'm going to a motel, I'm getting drunk, and tomorrow I'm finding a tavern where I can watch the Packers lose."

Bob stands in stunned silence.

"It's Sunday, goddamnit," I say, and I see something flicker in Bob's eyes.

"Coming?" I say.

Behind the trees, the group is being led in a chant.

Bob hangs back for a second, but only a second.

Then, he follows.

Help Wanted

The stranger pulls up on a motorcycle around eight, just as I'm finishing breakfast. Gail is at the front desk, her knitting needles running at a fast clip. I hear the man enter, the doorbells jingling, his boots scraping the floor. Gail bids him good morning and he does the same to her.

"What can I do for you today?" she asks. It's a bit early to receive new campers, but it happens.

"I wanted to find out if the job is still open," the man says, his voice gravel-rough. "The one posted off the roadside."

"Oh, you'll have to speak to my husband about that," Gail says. "Let me see if he's available."

Gail comes back and tells me about the inquiry. I push my plate to the side and come out to the registration office. I see an unshaven man with longish dark hair in a black T-shirt, blue jeans, and boots that look military issue. I don't recognize him, but I know the smell he gives off—cigarettes, a habit I quit fourteen years ago.

I shake a city-soft hand and introduce myself.

"Tom Westmore," I say, looking into the man's red-rimmed eyes. He seems surprised an old guy like me has such a hard grip.

"Dallas," he says.

"You from Texas?" I say, not detecting anything but Midwest in him.

"No sir," he says. "Chicago area, born and bred, but my father is from Texas."

"Hell, those summers are hot out there," I say. "Just been once to see the space center. Middle of July. Shoulda thought that one out better. Follow me, we can talk in back."

We sit in the room Gail and I outfitted to be both office and kitchen back in 1969 shortly after we bought the place. It hadn't changed much in the intervening years. Gail pours some coffee. She doesn't need to, but she starts puttering around so she can listen in, doing up the few dishes, then moving on to wiping the counter.

I get the man's story about how he lost his job as a baggage handler at O'Hare airport, how he's been living at Shady Lakes trailer park since two months past, how he wants to get back to work right here in Sutton if he can.

My former helper, Josh, moved to St. Louis when a job opened up at a rubber factory near the place where his cousin lives. Summer's coming on, and there's grass to cut. I've interviewed two people already, but they were unreliable locals who could only commit part-time. I need a full-time hand, and pretty quick.

I don't tell the stranger all of this, of course. Just the basic facts—that, mostly, the job is cutting grass, but it's also hauling trash, cleaning up the restrooms, and other odds and ends. It's twelve an hour, seven hours a day, five days a week.

The fella says this all sounds good to him, says he wants to work outdoors; long days are fine by him.

Something is triggering inside me during our talk, something that gives me a little pause. The fact this fella's not from around here, for one. The soft hands, for another. Nobody handles bags for a living and has such smooth hands.

I could check references, but that's not my way.

"You wanted by the law for anything?" I ask.

"Oh, for Pete's sake!" Gail says, spinning around. "Don't mind him!"

The man laughs. "No, that's fine," he says. "Truthfully, no. Want to see an ID card?"

He goes for his wallet, but I wave it away.

"That's all right," I say. "I didn't mean nothing by it. You ever in the service?" I ask, thinking about those boots.

"Yes, I was," the fella says. "Air Force during Desert Storm. Didn't see any action, though. They had me in Germany at an air base."

"No need to apologize for not fighting," I say. "It's overrated. I was in the Second World War. Navy," I say. I point to my gimpy leg. "Almost lost my leg to some shrapnel when we got torpedoed near Peleliu."

The man nods, and a pained look crosses his face.

"Anyway, the main thing with me is reliability. I need somebody here like clockwork. If you'll be out hootin' with the owls, I won't be able to use you. If you're steady and ready, well, I think this can work out."

"You won't have any problem with me," the fella says. "I promise you."

"Well, why don't we say we'll try you out for a week and see how it goes. We'll worry about form-filling later. What Uncle Sam don't know won't hurt him, the way I figure. Hell, it's more money in your pocket."

"Suits me," the man says.

A couple days later, the fella shows up at the agreed time. The sun is just coming over the horizon, a throbbing ball of flame.

"Looks to be a nice one, eh?" I say.

"Looking good," Fella agrees.

"Well how about we get right to it?" I say. "I figure we'll start by giving you a little tour of the grounds. For that job I got my trusty golf cart, Betty. Older I get, the less walking I do."

"Sounds fine."

We get into old Betty, and I take us past the RV sites first. I see Burt Dupree pulling up his awning, and I give him a wave as we go by. He waves back, his eyes following our wake.

"Most of the RVs are old-timers," I say. "They come in the spring and stay all summer, or most of it, anyway. Some come, some go, but we got quite a bit of regulars."

I move to the outer road, the one that pulls along Algonquin Lake.

"We got our tent sites over here," I say. "Twelve got electric, cost a few bucks more. Twelve others, primitives. Boat put-in is out that way."

Right now there are only four campers in the tent sites, but for mid-week, early spring, that's normal. It'll get busier soon enough.

"What's that building?" Fella says, pointing to the long, flat structure in the middle of the field.

"That's the rec room," I say. "Couple video games in there. A pinball. On Sundays we set up tables and Gail offers a cheap pancake breakfast to the campers."

"Nice."

"And that stuff all around the rec room," I say, "that's the grass that needs cutting. One thing we got a lot of, it's grass."

I show him the trash area, where the campers are expected to, but don't always, put their trash. I take him to the washrooms and showers and go over the cleaning of those. Then it's time for a lunch break.

"You're welcome to take an hour and go where you like," I say. "I'm sure you know what's in town. There's also Morgan's pub down on 78—they make a good half-pound burger. If you bring something in, we have a microwave in the office you can use. But, if you prefer, Gail will fix you up some sandwiches or leftovers for three bucks. You want her to prepare something, just let her know first thing so it's ready for you at noon. She's happy to oblige."

Today, Fella figures on trying one of those half-pound burgers, so he goes off on his bike. That gives me a chance to talk to Gail, who comes in as soon as he rides away.

"So, how was he?" she says.

"Quiet, but I think he'll pick up quick. Kind of an odd bird, though," I say.

"Why do you say that?"

"Dunno. Kinda twitchy."

"Oh, you're a fine one, Tom. You're just not used to him."

"Yeah, probably that's all," I say.

When he returns after lunch, I get the rider-mower out of the shed and demonstrate the operation. Within a few minutes he's off on the thing and I exhale, glad the job is finally getting done.

——⚬⚬⚬——

Before long, Fella (or Dallas, that is) is into a routine, and it's just in time. Registrations are pouring in.

Dallas takes his lunch mostly in the office, eating what Gail has for him. My initial concern about his reliability is put to rest, for the most part. Two weeks later, he's been on time every day and has done a solid job on the grass and the restrooms. The folks in the RVs are getting used to him, though nobody can seem to draw much conversation out of him.

"From Chicago, you said, Tom?" Burt Dupree asks me one afternoon. I'm sitting in the golf cart out in front of his RV, and we're talking about the Cubbies' prospects this year.

"How's that?" I say.

Dupree nods out towards Dallas, who's on the riding mower in the distance.

"Guess so," I say.

"How old you say he is?"

"Late twenties, early thirties, I'd guess," I say.

"You mean you don't know?" Dupree says. "What did he put on his application?"

"Don't know," I say. "We never got to filling one out."

"What about the tax forms? What'd he put on them?"

"We never got to filling those out either."

This information floors Dupree. He's a retired bookkeeper and can't stand the idea of breaking the law. We go back and forth on it until I finally tell him things will be legal soon enough.

"I should hope so, for your sake," Dupree says. "Last thing you need is the IRS on your doorstep."

"Yeah, hell. Anyways, I'll catch up with you later," I say. I spit in the dirt and drive off.

Next morning I tell Dallas we have to get these forms in.

"Forms?" he says.

He seems surprised, a little jittery, but by now I've got the idea that he likes to drink. It's probably from a hangover.

"W-4s and whatnot," I say. "I've been persuaded to get legal on this."

"Oh, of course," Dallas says. He goes over to the table and picks up the pen. As he fills out the paperwork, I notice his hand shaking a bit. When he's done, I see his given name, Dalton L. Boyd, in block lettering.

"Dalton, huh?" I say.

"Dallas is my nickname."

I put the papers on the counter and nod.

"That's all, then?" Dallas says.

"Yep, I guess that's all," I say.

Dallas pauses, and then finally ducks out the door. I remember something and call out from the porch door.

"Hey Dal, I almost forgot."

He stops and turns slowly.

"Yeah, what's that, boss?"

"Ice machine is almost out. Mind taking a run down to the Quick Mart and grabbing ten or so bags? Ice company isn't due for a couple days to refill our cooler. You can use the pickup."

"Sure, no problem."

Dallas comes back and gets the money and keys.

Out in the sun he looks even greener around the gills.

"Feeling all right?" I say.

"Oh yeah," he says. "Just not sleeping too great lately."

"OK," I say. I shut the screen door before more flies get in.

Later that night, Gail and I are having dinner, and she puts her pork sandwich down and shakes her head. "No, I shouldn't mention it," she says, more to herself than me.

"Mention what?"

"Oh nothing. Just Dallas. He came in before lunch with an unusual question."

"What question was that?"

"Oh, he asked if we had a father and son camping here. Says he saw them fishing behind one of the campsites this morning when he was picking up over there."

"Can't think of a boy here at the moment," I say. "How old?"

"He said about eight or nine years. Said they were wearing identical red plaid shirts and blue jeans."

"So, anybody here like that?" I say.

"No children right now," Gail says.

"Maybe they wandered in and threw a line," I say.

"That's what I thought too, and I told him, I said, you see them again, go ahead and ask if they're registered here," Gail says.

"Sometimes we get that," I say. "Sometimes. Not often. Not so unusual."

"But here's the strange part. Dallas said he approached them to ask how the fishing was, but by the time he got through the trees, they were gone. He couldn't imagine where they got off to, unless they jumped in the lake without making a splash."

I leave that alone. I don't like it, but there's nothing I can do with it. I shrug it off and we go on with dinner. Gail catches me up on what our daughter Sam is doing with her family in Bluff Springs—our grandson Jake's in Pee Wee baseball and our granddaughter Elaine is the best speller in her class.

A day or so later, I need Dallas to trim back some brush on one of the hiking paths that lead to the trails. When we meet up for lunch a few hours later, he comes in looking hollow-eyed, a bit panicked. He sits in front of his corned beef, but doesn't touch it.

"Something the matter?" I say, looking up from *Popular Mechanics*.

"I saw them again," he says.

"Who's that?"

"The other day I saw this father and son fishing behind campsite 4B. Maybe Gail told you?"

I nod.

"I saw them again. They were in the same place. Or, I thought they were. I went behind the trees, and somehow they got away from me again."

"Running? With poles and gear?"

Dallas wipes a hand over his forehead.

"No, they were just . . . *gone*."

Because there's just no way for a man and child to pull up lines and get away without someone seeing them do it—in a boat or on foot—I just pick up my sandwich.

"I'll keep an eye out," I say.

"I saw something," Dallas says. "I saw the name on their tackle box before they got away. *Sanders*, it said. Maybe you can check the registration log and see if we have anyone named Sanders here."

"Sure," I say. "Yep, I'll surely check on that."

After lunch I check and of course, there's no Sanders.

Around seven, I go for my nightly round of the campground on Betty. I dub this the "Victory Lap" and always smoke my "Victory Cigar" as I do it. It's a tradition I've done for years, the equivalent of tucking my campers into bed for the night.

As I make the go-round, I stop when I see Dupree outside with a can of Old Style in his hand and his basset hound, Skip, lying at his feet.

"Hey Dupe," I say. "How's tricks?"

"Cubbies got Farnsworth in," he says. "We're two runs up in the third."

"Glad to hear it," I say. Out by the lake, the bullfrogs are starting up.

"Say, you haven't seen any father-and-son team fishing behind the tent sites over there, maybe in the morning?" I say, pointing.

Dupree squints through the twilight, perking up. He loves any new intrigue, however small.

"No, can't say I have," he says. "Fishing isn't no good over there anyway. How come you ask?"

"Oh, my new guy thought he saw somebody over there a couple mornings. We don't have any kids registered right now, except that family in the Bronco that just come in this afternoon. They have two little ones."

"Worried they're gonna steal all the fish?" Dupree says.

I make a sour face.

"If they're not registered here, they're trespassing."

"I'll keep a lookout for ya, how's that?" Dupree says.

"Much obliged."

"Say, you ever get that fella's full name, the one working for you?"

"Dalton Boyd," I say.

"Boyd, that's Irish, isn't it?"

"I suppose. Yeah, probably."

"So I take it he's legal now?"

"Legal as Christmas," I say.

"Glad to hear it."

Dupree leans back, sips off his beer.

I look round the campground. Night is falling fast.

"Well, I gotta scoot," I say. "Good night, now."

"Good night."

I make the rest of the circle silently, not disturbing anybody. Fires are sprouting up, filling the air with the comforting smell of wood smoke.

A bit later I'm having my own cerveza on the porch with Gail, who's reading one of her crime thrillers. The ember on the mosquito coil is burning around its spiral. I'm staring through the screen at the moon; it's half-full tonight.

"What are you thinking about?" Gail asks.

"I guess I'm thinking of our new helper," I say.

"He's a bit of a drinker, yah?" she says.

"Herb Talbot told me he drank Morgan's to closing several times, so I suppose that's the case," I say.

"He's been gobblin' up the aspirin in the washroom here," Gail says. "Like nobody's business."

I nod. "He's young, still," I say. "When I was his age, I was still kickin' my demons out."

"I remember."

"He brought up that business with the father and son again," I say. "Same thing. Says he saw them and then they vanished."

Gail rests her book in her lap.

"He said he got a look at the name printed on their tackle box. Sanders, it said. I checked. No Sanders here. So I asked Dupe if he saw anybody fishin' over by the tent sites and he said he hasn't seen anybody."

"Maybe it's the booze," Gail says. "It can cause hallucinations, you know."

I shake the dregs of my beer around in the bottom of the can, looking down the dark hole in the top.

"Well, if it's hallucinations," I say, "he better start scheduling them for after work hours. I don't have time for nonsense."

The rest of the week goes by without incident—at least nothing is reported to Gail or me. Dupree has been eagle-eyeing campsite 4B for fishermen, but there's nothing from him either. I'm figuring this is all behind us when, one afternoon, I hear Dupree come into the office and say how-do to Gail. He wanders to the back, where I'm fiddling with a busted lock.

"Hey Dupe," I say, looking up. "To what do I owe the esteemed honor?"

It's a joke between me and Gail that Dupe wouldn't leave his RV if a tornado was coming right at it.

"Your fella Boyd," he says. "He's over at 4B. Got himself a fire going over there."

"What?" I say.

"Have a look-see yourself."

I put the lock down and ask Gail if we have anybody in 4B.

"No one there right now," she says, checking the log.

I come outside, with Dupree following, and look across the field. I can make out Dallas in the distance, standing in front of a fire.

"Paying folks to watch fire?" Dupree says. "If so, I want that job."

"Goddamnit!" I say. "What the hell?"

Gail comes outside too. "Now, don't rush to judgment," she says, but I'm already getting in the cart and tearing off, my mind boiling.

When I get close, I see that the fire pit is jammed full with enough wood to keep it going for three hours. There's no trace of kindling or extra pieces of wood anywhere, only the fire blazing and popping.

Dallas jumps a bit when he realizes I'm behind him.

"Somebody set a fire over here," he says, gesturing to the flames.

"I can see that," I say.

Dallas looks at me, his eyes sick with fear.

"Nobody on 4B," I say. "So who do you suppose did this?" We're both standing so close to the fire, we're perspiring.

"I—I don't know. I saw it as I was coming in on the rider. No one was here tending it, so I came over to investigate."

I look at Dallas's eyes and they can't hold mine for more than a second. He looks back at the fire, disconcerted. He shakes his head. "It's the damnedest thing," he says.

"Well, that's good wood in there," I say. "Looks like twenty dollars' worth. Best put it out so we can reuse some of it, don't you think?"

"Yeah, right," Dallas says.

"I'd drag out the hose from the rec house," I say. "Make the job go a mite quicker."

Dallas nods and starts off for the rec house. I slap at a mosquito landing on my arm and drive Betty back.

Next morning I only see Dallas first thing as he's punching in. If it's possible, he looks worse than usual. Rings under his eyes like he hasn't slept a wink, but I don't have much sympathy.

"I'm off to Traynor. I'll be gone most of the day," I tell him. "Those showers could really use a swab-down. Can you see to that before lunch?"

"Sure. No problem," Dallas says, his voice dry as sandpaper. Voice of a late night with one cigarette after another.

"Hey, Boss," he says, just as I'm about to go. We're both on the porch. His forehead is creased in the center, a deep ravine of worry. "I didn't burn up that wood, just so you know, but I'll find out who did."

"Don't worry nothing about that," I say, waving it away. "Got lots else to worry about than wood, believe me."

I get in the pickup and pull out to the highway. I gun it hard and fast, windows down, taking my aggression out in speed.

I spend a leisurely day in Traynor, shopping and kicking around. I go to the Farm and Fleet and pick up some overalls, some fishing lures, and other odds and ends, then head over to the bank to make a deposit. I take lunch at Bransford's counter, then head over to Brady's Lounge for a beer and spend some time bullshitting with Dale Brady, the owner. By three o'clock I'm back in the pickup with a couple DQ fudge sundaes, racing to get home before they melt.

When I get back, Gail is in the office signing in some new campers: two brothers from Ohio, judging by their looks and the plates on their Honda. Once Gail has them squared away, she dips her plastic spoon into the sundae I set in front of her.

"I've been looking forward to this all day," she says. "You have no idea."

"I hurried back," I say. "I tried to keep 'em out of the sun as much as I could."

"Oh, it's delicious."

I look out at the field and don't see the mower moving about.

"Dallas around someplace?" I say. "Patch of grass by the cornfield is almost a foot high. I can see it from here."

Gail shakes her head. "No, he asked to go home early," she says.

"What time was that?" I say.

"Around noon. Right after he got upset about this piece of paper he found."

I put the ice-cream cup down.

"Piece of paper?" I say. "What paper?"

"He said he was picking up that wood from yesterday and he found something in the coal dust. Said it looked like an airline ticket, mostly burnt up. It really upset him, I don't know why."

My blood runs hot, then cold, and my hands start to clench reflexively. It's lucky Dallas isn't here, because I'd certainly be giving him hell over this.

"He in tomorrow?" I say.

"You gave him this weekend off," Gail says.

I slap the armrest of the wicker futon couch with the flat of my palm.

"I hired a mental patient!" I say. "For christsakes!"

"I'm sure there's an explanation," Gail says.

"I'm sure there is," I say. "And I'm going to get it from him tomorrow. You betcha."

I toss the rest of my ice cream in the trash and go upstairs.

Next day, as I'm preparing to make a visit over to Shady Lakes trailer park, I run into Dupree, who's got a too-wide smile on his old puckered face and some papers in his hand.

"Morning sir!" he calls. I shut off the sprinklers going at the garden out back.

"Hey Dupe, morning to you."

"Got a minute?" he says.

"Sure, I got a minute. But not much more."

"Got something to show ya," Dupree says. "Someplace we can sit down and talk for a moment?"

I gesture to the tool shed, where there are a couple stumps behind we can sit on.

"I made a trip over to the library yesterday," Dupree says, still concealing the papers in his hands. "You'll never guess what I found on their Internet computer."

"You're right," I say, "I won't." Half the world has been sucked into their cell phones, computers, and music pods. I'm not going too.

Dupree unfolds his papers and snaps his forefinger at the front page. It's a photocopy of *The Chicago Tribune* from a few months back.

AIR-TRAFFIC CONTROLLER DESCRIBES EVENTS THAT LED TO DEADLY CRASH

He points a crooked finger to a line he's highlighted.

"This your boy?" he says. "Dalton L. Boyd?"

I skim over the article and start remembering hearing about this on the news. An air-traffic controller got confused about how many planes he had coming in and allowed one to land on an occupied runway. Thirty-nine people died as a result. There's no photo of Dalton, but his name is there, plain as day.

Some things start getting clearer now, like the fact Dallas's hands were as soft as foam before he began here. Makes sense if all he was doing was pushing buttons and speaking into an intercom. Some other things start to make sense too.

As I go over the article, my leg starts to ache. I want Dupree to go away now. I need to think on this.

"Can I keep these?" I say.

"Sure, keep 'em. What are you gonna do?"

"Leave that to me," I say. "Meanwhile, keep your pie hole shut about this."

—⁂—

When I show up at Shady Lakes trailer park, I go to the main office, an elevated trailer with an American flag on top. Jack Ford is at his desk inside, talking a mile a minute on his phone to some creditor. When he's through, he hangs up and asks me how's biz. Thing about Jack is, he's always been competitive.

"So-so," I say. "Can't complain."

"How's that fella working out?" he says. "Dallas."

"Just fine," I say. "I need to speak to him about something, actually. Mind pointing me in the right direction?"

"Trailer 75," Jack says. "Just follow along that road there and hook a left by the restrooms. Want me to take you?"

"No, I got it from here, thanks."

I walk the road slowly, feeling the pain whiz up my leg. To either side, dirty-faced kids are running around playing with busted plastic toys, their parents nowhere to be seen.

A wooden post marks trailer 75. The gray windows are covered with bed sheets.

I knock on the screen door, rattling it in its frame. After a minute, I hear some stirring and cursing. A piece of cloth moves off the door window and Dallas peeks through, his hair mussed like he's just woken.

"Hey Tom, what's up?"

"Think we can speak for a minute?" I say.

"If it's about yesterday . . . I'm sorry I left early," he says. "I wasn't feeling too good."

"That's OK," I say. "All right if I come in a second?"

Dallas looks behind him at something. "Tom, really, you probably shouldn't."

"Just five minutes," I say. "My leg needs a rest."

Reluctantly, Dallas opens the door and reveals a living area covered in forests of empty liquor bottles, pizza boxes, cigarette packs, and dirty plates.

"I'm telling you, this place is a mess," he says.

"Never mind about that," I say, coming in. Dallas removes some old newspapers from a ratty chair and clears a space for himself. The threadbare couch has cigarette burns along the arm rests. He puts a hand through his hair to comb it down.

"Can I get you a coffee or something?" he asks, motioning toward a kitchen that looks like it was hit with a mortar.

"No, I'm fine, thanks."

"This must look pretty horrible," Dallas says. "I'm sorry about this."

"I didn't come here to lecture you about cleanliness habits," I say. "I came here because I know about what happened to you. I know about the *accident*."

Dallas' face goes from choppy to still.

"You weren't just handling bags at O'Hare, you were handling the planes that carried those bags . . . and those people," I say.

Dallas nods. I can hear a clock ticking in the kitchen.

"Any of this have to do with what's going on with you at the campground?"

Dallas looks down at his hands and shakes his head.

"I don't know . . . possibly. Things have been happening. Things I can't explain," he says. "You know that name I saw on the tackle box? What if I told you that was the name of a man and his son who got killed on one of those planes?"

"What if it was? Sanders is a common enough name."

"I checked with my former boss at the airport. He has the seating chart to the plane. The names of the deceased. Jeffrey Sanders sat in seat 4B, the same number as the campsite. He and his son burned alive because of me. What do you make of that?"

Dallas gets up suddenly and goes to the kitchen. He comes back with a piece of paper and hands it to me. "Look at this."

I'm holding what appears to be a ticket of some kind, but it's mostly burnt up, illegible.

"It's just a piece of paper," I say.

"It's an airline ticket," Dallas says. "I found it in the remains of the fire the other day. Same colors United uses."

I put the paper down because this I cannot believe, and yet something else can't be denied.

"You've been through a trauma," I say. "All you're doing, you're living it over again. It's normal, this kind of thing."

Dallas looks across the room, rejoining the day that destroyed his life.

"One minute I was in the tower and everything was fine, and, the next, there's a fireball on the runway. Firemen and rescue personnel are running out there and I'm still in my chair, still controlling the other planes, telling them we have a problem here, don't land. I had no idea at first that I'd *caused* it."

Dallas shakes his head and wipes away a tear streaming down his face.

I clear my throat because I have my own story to tell, something I haven't told but a few times to a few people.

"Indulge me a minute, can you?" I say.

Dallas nods.

I tell him about Peleliu, about how my Navy buddy Harris and I were captured by the Japanese and put in a holding tank on a ship with twenty-five other guys, men who were half-starved, dying of thirst and heat exhaustion. I describe for him the craziness men had for water, liquid of any kind, how they'd try to bite your neck for blood. How this caused me and Harris to take turns watching over each other to try to survive down there.

I illustrate the night I accidentally fell asleep on watch and a skeleton of a man came up and took a chunk out of Harris's neck, causing him to go apeshit. The Japanese guards opened the hatch above and sprayed us down with bullets, one of which caught Harris behind the ear and killed him. Four others were dead besides.

I talk about my guilt over causing those deaths, and the long days that passed afterwards.

"Finally, on the fourth day, the Japs throw a rope down so they can haul the dead bodies out, and when it comes Harris's turn, they take him all the way up and stop there and let him spin around. He just kept looking down at us with a grin that may as well have been permanently stamped on my eyeballs. I used to see him everywhere—in my closet, on the side of the road, in my dreams all the time. I won't kid you. Sixty years later, I still see Harris spinning around in front of my bed sometimes."

I pick up the paper ticket lying there. From another world or not, for Dallas it is what he thinks it is.

"I guess what I'm saying is, bad things can happen to a fella, and it ain't easy, but you gotta try to put it behind you. You can't pack it away, but you don't have to live with these people standing in your way either. They're dead. You're alive. So *live*. It was just their time. It was a mistake. We can't change what's done."

The clock ticks on a half minute with Dallas staring a hole into the carpet.

I figure I've said what I came to say. It will help or it won't; it's not my call to make. I stand up and put a hand on Dallas's shoulder.

"I hope you don't run off, Dallas. Gail and I need you. Keepin' busy is the best thing, trust me."

Dallas looks up and nods. "Thanks, Tom."

"Well, I'll be going, then."

I let myself outside and start toward the car, head bent to the gravel, my leg aching with every step.

Protector

In the night, crime lurks.

Seth takes a white pill from a small oval case in his vest. He swallows it back with a swig of tonic water and wonders who he'll save tonight, what justice he'll deliver. He walks to the red light district of the city. Friday night. People are out to have some fun: women laughing, cars honking, street lights flashing, neon, sounds of music from club doors. He stands on a small traffic island in the middle of the chaos. Citizens step onto it, wait for green, and then pass on. He stays there, surveying the scene, looking for signals.

On one of the six corners, a homeless man is hawking his poems, rattling sheets at passersby.

"One dolla . . . one dolla . . . pomes, one dolla . . ."

At another corner, a gang of street toughs walks by in puffy jackets, their jeans scraping along the sidewalk, their heads close-cropped. They are sixteen going on forty.

"Hey, buddy!"

Seth turns. The speaker is a young man in his twenties; a cigarette dangles from his lips. "Gotta light?"

Seth's lips curl in distaste. "Smoking stinks," he says.

The man is unfettered. He moves on and is swallowed up by the street in seconds.

Seth scans the apartments above; some are brightly lit with people moving inside. Parties, a tattoo parlor, a cat. No signs of disturbance. No man forcibly raping a woman. No murderer wielding an ax in sharp relief. He flexes and feels his muscles ripple beneath his utility clothing.

A police car goes by. It looks puny and comical—a cardboard man driving a tin vehicle, a foil badge on his chest, following rules written in some law book somewhere. Laughable.

Seth moves to the El line and pays for a ride he will not take. He climbs the stairs to the platform overlooking the six corners and moves toward the far edge where there are ample shadows. He can view the activity on the platform from this vantage, while also getting a bird's eye view of the street.

El cars roll up. When they do, Seth looks inside the yellow boxes and surveys the situation. He sees no one snatching necklaces, no one waving a gun. No one harassing a woman.

The platform fills up with people, many of them loud and obnoxious. Seth monitors them. When he sees a drunken woman getting too close to the edge, he steps between her and the rails.

"Behind the line for safety," he says. The woman laughs uproariously and moves back with her companion.

Seth returns to the street and positions himself outside a 24-hour hot-dog joint. When a Lincoln Town Car pulls to a stop, he grabs the handle of the passenger door and opens it.

The man in the driver's seat is startled.

"Hey! What the fuck—?"

"You should lock your doors," Seth says sternly. He slams the door shut. He does this twice more, then notices he's attracting attention, which defeats his purpose. He moves down the block, past restaurants and bars, and goes into a bar packed full of people. Music is blaring. Seth elbows his way to the bar and orders a tonic water.

"Vodka tonic?" the barmaid says.

"Tonic only."

He pays and walks among the crowd. Everyone is cloistered into little groups and talking animatedly. Seth observes the sign posted behind the bar that defines the capacity limits, and does some quick math. He envisions a stampede for the door, people crushing each other, suffocating. He moves to the bar. The barmaid strains to hear him. Seth is pointing to the sign.

"Over capacity . . . too many people here . . ."

"What? Are you a cop?"

"No. But there's too many people here."

"Whatever." The barmaid moves on. Ten people want a drink from her.

Seth goes to the entrance. A doorman is sitting on a stool. Even his head looks like a muscle.

"The bar is over capacity," Seth says.

The doorman looks behind him. "We always have this many people here."

"Then you're always over capacity. People could get hurt."

"Did you get hurt?"

"No."

"Then kiss my ass. I'm not the manager."

Seth continues down the street. In the parking lot of a fast food restaurant he sees nine Latino teenagers taking turns beating on a boy who is crouched in self-defense.

"Bitch! Pussy bitch! Nigga!"

Sounds of flesh hitting flesh.

Seth's adrenaline rises. His veins feel full of molten steel. His head hums.

"Excuse me."

The youths turn to look at him.

"Stop hitting that boy."

A mutt-faced gang-banger with a scarred eyebrow smiles.

"Fuck off, bitch. Ain't your business."

"Stop hitting the boy," Seth says again.

The blow connects to the deepest region of his stomach. He doubles over and falls to the pavement. A bottle is thrown at him, almost hitting his head. Someone spits on him.

Seth limps away. His hand is bleeding where it landed in some broken glass. He enters an all-night diner. Many in the room turn to look at him. A washed-out woman is staffing the grill. The smell of bacon and grease mixes with cigarette smoke.

Seth pulls some napkins out of a dispenser to stanch the blood flow, sits down, and orders a water.

"Anything to eat?"

"Just the water."

The woman frowns. "If you just want water, that's gonna be a dollar."

Seth pulls out a crumpled dollar and lays it on the countertop. The water is delivered, choked with ice. Seth takes another pill. He will be better in a few minutes.

There is a pretty woman dining alone at a table by the window. She looks at Seth and smiles. Seth takes his water over and sits down across from her. The woman stops smiling.

"Excuse me," Seth says. "I just need to sit down."

The woman shakes her head. "You were sitting down over there."

"Lot of crazy activity tonight," Seth says.

"Oh, yeah?"

"Definitely."

"Where were you, at a party or something?"

"No, just out and about."

The woman nods and finishes her coffee. She smiles again, briefly.

"Well, good night."

She stands up and gathers her purse. Seth follows her out the door.

"Hey, do you need an escort?" Seth says.

"A what?"

"An escort? Someone to protect you tonight?"

The woman smiles and rolls her eyes.

"No thank you, I'm fine."

She stops at the corner bus stop.

"It's dangerous in the city for a young woman."

"How old are you?"

"Twenty-four."

"The city can be dangerous for you, too."

Seth holds up his bleeding hand. "I know. But I have to."

"You have to, what?"

"Nothing. I have to be here. I have to protect you."

The woman looks for her bus. "I'm fine, I'm fine. Look, there are people all around. Now, why don't you go home and take care of that hand?"

The bus arrives and, against her protests, Seth gets on. He takes the seat behind her. The woman sighs audibly.

"I'm Seth. That's my real name," he says.

"I'm Wanda. That's my fake name."

"I understand. Can't be too careful."

The bus goes north. Seth watches the faces of the other passengers. One gives him the finger, and Seth looks away. Several stops later, the woman stands up and Seth gets up to follow her. She turns quickly and puts up her hand.

"Don't," she says. "No farther. Go home." She exits the bus, and Seth leaps off behind her. They've walked about a half block when the woman turns suddenly and sprays Seth in the face with pepper spray. Then she turns and runs as Seth drops to his knees, blinded.

He has no money for a cab, so he walks back toward the red-light district. At an alleyway, a woman in a scant outfit of polyester top and shorts approaches him.

"Come here, Mr. Man. Is Mr. Man horny tonight?"

Seth stomps off, ignoring her.

A half hour later, he is back in the chaos. Bars are spilling customers into the street. Cabs are transporting them home. Seth sits in the doorway of a building, monitoring as much as he can until his eyes can no longer stay open.

Dawn breaks and he is lying supine in the doorway. His throat is parched, his head fuzzy. He shields his eyes against the streaking daylight and feels in his pocket for his pills, but finds they're gone.

As he passes by, Desmond, the poetry hawker, stops him.

"Guardian! Hey, Guardian!"

Seth turns.

Desmond palms him a Dexie and winks.

"Rough night, huh? That'll get ya home. On the house, bro."

Seth swallows the pill dry. Desmond smiles.

"See you again tonight, Guardian? Yeah, right. This 'hood need its protector."

Seth nods groggily and moves towards home.

Desmond rattles pages in the air. "Pomes! One dolla for a pome!"

The Actor

They were filming a movie in town, the newspaper said, and it was going to feature an actor whom Sandy loved.

"Oh my God," she said to her husband, Jay. "I've got to go. He's going to be right here, filming his new movie!"

Jay sighed. Since he'd been with Sandy, she'd talked about Vic Lynch and her love of him many times. He'd always regarded this with detached amusement, but that had been before, when Lynch had just been an image on a screen and not a real person who was soon to be walking around Chicago.

A cloud passed over Jay's face and Sandy chose to disregard it, because this love she had for Lynch was make-believe love: the kind that anyone with imagination had access to. It wasn't the hard-fought kind that happened between real people, the kind that was made up of gradual getting-to-know-you experiences, the two would-be lovers moving toward each other from opposite sides of a steep hill before planting a mutually declared flag at the top.

"Oh, he's going to be near Bucktown, shooting," Sandy said as she read on, her eyes sucking at the print details like Dirt Devils. "Maybe I'll take Thursday off. Call in sick and go see if I can meet him."

Jay rattled the spoon around his tea and rubbed his whiskered chin. Was it normal to put celebrity obsession over work? Of course it wasn't normal. It was practically stalking.

"You want to get his autograph or something?" Jay said.

Sandy's eyes flashed. "Oh, *absolutely*," she said.

"Really? You're going to take the day off and stand around hoping he comes out of his trailer?"

"You can come if you want," Sandy said. "I was going to ask Connie to go. Connie loves him too."

Did Connie *really*? Jay wondered what Connie would say if, right now, he called and asked her. It would be weird, but he'd get a straight answer. Most likely, she didn't love Lynch all that much; Sandy would ask Connie to come mainly so that Jay wouldn't. He didn't like Connie, particularly her fried blonde hair and the way she laughed huskily at her own jokes.

"Do what you want," Jay said. He rinsed out his teacup.

The following day, Sandy called in sick and went downtown with Connie. They spent the better part of the day watching despondent movie-truck operators and construction hands position lights, cables, and other equipment, and relentlessly quizzing them in attempts to divulge details about Lynch's whereabouts and proclivities.

"What kind of cigarette does he smoke?"

"Are there any bars you think he might go to while he's here? Any sights he wants to see?"

Though she didn't get a chance to meet Lynch, and actually hadn't even gotten so much as a look at him all day, Sandy returned home ecstatic. "It was great just being near all the Hollywood production stuff," she said. "Knowing he was there was terribly exciting."

She was going back tomorrow, she said.

"Really? Is it worth all this?" he asked.

"Oh yeah," Sandy said. "Definitely."

The next day she went again, but this time to a new location on North Michigan Avenue. She went alone, since Connie had a dental appointment. This time, Sandy actually managed to see Lynch do a scene. She was far away from the action and the crowds were kept well behind a barricade, but nonetheless, there he was—Vic Lynch, in the flesh, doing a scene. She wished she could have heard his voice, but the distance between them was too great.

"He's gorgeous!" Sandy later exclaimed to Jay, as she rifled through the paper and found an article about the movie, which, apparently, had to do with gangsters.

"Wow—he's doing all his own stunts," she said. "The director, D. Scott, has tried to convince him not to, but he *insists*! Isn't that crazy?"

"Yeah, real crazy," Jay said, squinting at the sports section.

"You know," Sandy said, "I got some inside information yesterday from one of the security guys. I kept joking with him, and he might have taken a shine to me or something. He told me that the stars were going out to Hanna's Bar this weekend. I was thinking maybe I'd go down there and see if I can meet him in person."

When she put her mind to something, Sandy didn't stop until it was accomplished. She had an obsessive/compulsive streak.

"Why don't we both go?" Jay said.

Sandy hesitated. "Well . . . sure," she said. "That could be fun."

On Saturday evening at about nine-thirty, Sandy and Jay got dressed up and went downtown. Part of Jay hoped this foray would be nothing more than a wild goose chase with a couple of martinis thrown on top, but another part of him wanted to meet Lynch up close, have a good look at him, and demystify him once and for all. He was just another human being, after all. He had to die someday too. He might do it on sheets with a six-hundred-plus thread count, but he'd die just the same. Death wouldn't forget about him.

Hanna's was an uber-posh, low-lit swankery with butter-soft leather seats and a lighted, curling bar that led out to the patio. It was staffed by a cadre of professionals who seemed superior in every way except that they were bartenders. They looked like magicians with their crisp white button-down shirts and black bow ties, as they executed drink making with a dexterous skill that could make a person dizzy.

Jay ordered two gin martinis and tried to conceal his shock when he learned the price. He looked around. Everywhere, fabulous-looking people were practically shimmering with life and laughter. They were alive and wholly unconcerned, and twenty dollars a drink did not bother them in the slightest. They had scads of money, and their money didn't just sit there, either. Their money *did* stuff. It was acrobatic. Their money had skills. Their money *made* money.

"Come on," Sandy said. "Let's go towards the back."

She pulled Jay by the hand, slicing through the crowd like a speedboat parting a lake. They slid to a stop near the terminus of the bar, which ended in a dazzling outdoor cleft near some very tall palm-like plants. Somehow, the patio bar was even more fabulous than the indoor portion.

They found a spot along the rail, and Sandy started talking to a young woman in a black dress and her fiancé, a tall man with overgelled hair.

"So if you were taking a night off from the grueling film schedule, wouldn't you come *here*?" Sandy asked the couple. They agreed. Sandy sipped her cocktail. "It's like being on hunt for lions," she said. "You have to go to the river where they drink. It's the only way to get close to them."

They made their martinis and conversation last, but eventually Jay had to re-up their order, and Sandy grew bored of the young couple, who seemed only to want to talk about their impending marriage. They were like tropical fish: nice to look at, but not all that fun to engage.

Sandy turned and started talking to a rotund man whose suspenders and gold pinkie ring bespoke of back-room deals with politicos. He had defended high-profile clients in the city, he said, most notably a south-side alderman involved in a prostitution ring and a young man who'd been caught in the subway with explosives.

"Ever seen any celebrities here?" Sandy asked him.

"Oh, sure. In the '70s I saw Cheryl Tiegs. Sugar Ray Leonard. Those boys from ZZ Top. Oh, and Ozzy Osbourne once, crocked out of his gourd on Courvoisier. He was dressed like a nurse for some reason."

Sandy rubbed her hands together.

"I'm feeling it," she confided to Jay. "Aren't you?"

Jay shrugged and headed to the washroom, an architectural wonder with marble sinks, flat-screen TVs for every self-flushing urinal, and an elderly black attendant who watched over silver trays full of mints, chewing gum, deodorants, colognes, chocolates, and roses. For a few dollars, anyone could pull off a magic act in this washroom.

When Jay returned from the men's room, he presented a rose to Sandy.

"Where did this come from?" she asked, happily accepting it. She was now talking to someone Jay at first took to be one of the club managers. The fellow was dressed mostly in black and had a wide-open-neck collar, no tie. Rings on almost every finger. Long dark waves of hair.

The man's obsidian eyes roamed over Sandy, who had opted for a generous showing of cleavage tonight, and his smile flashed white and wide as he laughed at something she said. It was only then Jay realized this was Lynch.

Sandy was talking at light speed, her hand gestures manic as she scrambled to contain herself. Jay felt himself borne away in her exo-flood of emotion, grinning like a dumbass and holding a camera to snap a shot of his wife hugging, now kissing this son-of-a-bitch on the cheek.

Lynch shook hands with Jay, a brief handshake that somehow disconnected Jay even further.

"My husband, Jay," Sandy said, like he was an old automobile she'd meant to replace a long time ago for something sleek, handsome, and sporty.

"Delighted," Lynch said, accepting a drink compliments of the bar. Sandy looked like her legs were melting.

Jay wanted to punch. Wanted to hit things. What if this joker was single? What if this jewel of humanity just said—and his vocal cords were capable of it, certainly—what if he said to Sandy: *Let's go over to my hotel.* What would she do?

Jay imagined how she'd make excuses for it, would promise Jay she wouldn't do anything, that she'd just have a drink. Or maybe, feeling reckless, she *wouldn't* promise, but would instead whisper that, if he let her do this one thing, if he granted her this one eternal wish, then he, Jay could have whatever he wanted along those lines as well.

While his mind was grappling with this hypothetical conversation, he felt his attention magnetically pulled toward a blonde. Was that Faye Campbell in the corner? Yes, definitely, no mistaking her. Here was one of the few actresses who actually held some power over him. She was older, sure, but still beautiful, still smoldering. Maybe she was in the gangster picture too. If so, Sandy had neglected to mention it.

Faye saw him staring and smiled back. She gave her fruit-laden drink a twirl with her straw and waggled her delicate fingers at him. What thoughts were forming behind those minx-like eyes?

One more second and Jay might have answered the beckoned call, and what happened after that would have been in fate's hands. He took one small step, almost imperceptible. He was already stuttering. Already stammering. Oh God, those eyes, those sly lips!

And Sandy stole Jay's hand into hers. Clamping it tightly in a death grip, she apologized to Mr. Delightful. From far away, Jay heard her say, "We can't wait for the movie! It was a pleasure to meet you, but we really have to be going."

She turned quickly and snatched the rose from the top of the bar. Using it like a truncheon, she cast bodies aside as they made their way to the exit to locate the valet.

Dolls

I don't know what my previous lives were like.

I only know that I have awakened.

I've emerged from a shell while others continue to sleep. I travel in the half light. It's dangerous out here. There are animals. Sounds. Things that will attack. The early morning seems safest, so I travel then, slowly, just a bit each day.

For days I've traveled, seeing nothing—no animals—but now, each day, there are more. Some crawl; some bound; some glide, gallop, or fly.

Sometimes things change before my eyes. A mountain appears or disappears in the distance. The ground beneath me changes from sand to rock to grass. I eat what seems to be edible from the plants around me. I'm lucky there has been water.

When I sleep, I enter a more structured world. Things aren't under construction there like they are here. I close my eyes and I see other people—people who claim to know me, whom I have some kind of relationship with. These people speak to me familiarly. They have shelters lined up side by side in rows.

In this dream world, I'm clothed in fine clothing. A woman is close to me. My heart pulls at the sight of her, but I don't know her name.

The world builds itself in my peripheral vision. Roots tunnel and intermingle. Entire fields turn to dust and then to forest. The sun is the only constant. The huge glob in the sky burns me into the shelter of caves and hollows.

Days ago, I knew less.

When I first woke, I stumbled in a stupor. I'm not sure I could even walk. My knees were scabbed. I may have crawled. It's fortunate that the animals came later; I would surely have been prey by now.

But I'm learning things. Somehow, information comes into my head—the rate is ever accelerating. I've used tools. I've learned to trap animals. I've discovered fire.

But this is not really true. I woke up one day and I *knew* about fire. I knew how to kill animals. I knew how to clothe myself and build shelter.

Recently I've been seeing new things. In my wanderings, I've been seeing structures, amazing unnatural things, and not just in my dreams. I've been seeing rigid forms build up before my eyes.

I know some of their names.

There's a half-finished playground with iron bars, a slide, a swing set. Some bars stretch out to nothing. Some chains dangle without a seat. Some things are invisible.

Other structures. *Buildings.* Brick and glass, half-formed. A police station, a library, a prison, a deli. These are new concepts to me, but I know them like I've always known them.

For two days, maybe longer, I was seeing signs; billboards on roads that stretched themselves into limitless distance. I wasn't able to understand them.

And then, overnight, I knew what the word-symbols meant.

Number One Relief Medicine.

News Radio 780.

Helzberg Diamonds.

The next day, the city is more here than ever. An immovable lake. Bridges, post office, elevated train tracks. No people yet—just these things sprouting up.

I know about an important fire. A legend involving a cow and a lantern.

Who is whispering to me while I sleep?

Can you tell me how I learned to read? To add?

Can you tell me how I learned about Einstein and Thomas Jefferson?

Yesterday there was no Van Gogh. Now, how could anyone *not* know who he is?

I'm not in Europe, have never been to Europe. But I know all about Europe. About World War II.

I've never seen a war.

A haze settles on the city. I know this is pollution. There are cigarette butts and smashed paper cups along the expressways, but there's no one here yet to have thrown them down.

I miss people I have never met.

I miss my wife, whom I have never spoken to, never held.

Valerie.

Life isn't necessarily better with penicillin and mirrors, but it's certainly more comfortable.

Television fills in the gaps. It tells me all about this world yet to be born.

I would've learned about it anyway without television. As I've said, things come to me. But television speeds things up.

Song lyrics. A comic book I cherished. My first girlfriend. A trip to Wyoming. Books. Birthdays. All this comes crowding in without introduction.

This is my life, I'm finding out.

I've just learned my own name.

It's Daniel Crenshaw.

I'm half German, one-quarter English, one-quarter Irish.

I've lived in Chicago for ten years, and yet I've just arrived.

There are no deadly animals here, but I'm wary of eyes anyway. I understand that maybe I've escaped something, or have been released but shouldn't have been, so I stay indoors, mostly. In the city, it's easy to go from building to building or to travel underground until I find out where everyone else is.

Meanwhile, the pyramids are 4,000 years old and the Civic Opera House is nearing completion. Hitler is dead and there's an oil embargo. The murder rate appears to be dropping.

At Union Station I find some answers. Or, more questions. Here I'm miniaturized by the cavernous hall. An American flag the size of a house hangs near the glass ceiling, which lets in entirely too much light. I find humans lined up like dolls in cellophane, leaning against marble columns and long wooden benches. All ages, all sizes, all waiting to be born.

I understand that I was loosed; my box was opened prematurely. I wasn't meant to see all this; wasn't meant to roam like this.

The past is just finishing up now. The library shelves are full. It's almost time for the future to start.

Why it doesn't occur to me sooner, I don't know. Maybe I like exploring other people's empty houses, picking through their closets and photo albums. I find a telephone book. I look myself up.

I live at 4600 N. Winchester.

On my way, I think I know what I'll find: a modest home with a small, manicured lawn. A Ford Escort in the driveway.

In the last day or so, while the paint has dried on the parking spaces and the carpets have been getting tacked down, my identity has come crashing through.

I'm a systems technician for a candy manufacturer.

A perfect evening to me is dinner and a movie.

I'm a Sox fan.

I enter my home with a key I suddenly have, and I think about how I have to get the WD-40 and spray the hinge on that creaking door already. How the bathroom tile needs replacing, how I should stop putting off getting that wisdom tooth pulled.

I fill my future dog's dish full of food and crawl into bed next to my wife, who stirs but does not wake.

At 7:00 a.m. the alarm clock erupts and the world is blisteringly alive. Sirens are screaming, traffic is hissing, there are voices, an electric hum in the air.

I shave the beard off my face and the last of the old world goes spiraling down the sink. I only have a moment to kiss Valerie before I have to dash off to catch my train, a coffee clenched in my fist.

At work it is Monday, December 2nd, the first day of everything. No one notices how fresh the world really is, because somehow it's coated up in ages of grime. Kids are obese. Nuclear rods are unsecured. Space flight is routine. The ozone is half-gone.

Newspaper microfilm reels go back to the 1700s, as if anyone was around back then to do anything of the things that got reported as news. Dead celebrities are wound up on films that never got made.

JFK was never shot.

JFK did not exist.

All day long my coworkers say I look different. Is there something different about me?

They have no idea.

Chili

For one night and one night only, Kenneth Jackson's famous chili enabled some people in Taggert County to speak to the dead. Who could say exactly what proportions of meat, onion, garlic, tomato sauce, chili powder, sweet pepper, basil, kidney beans, Tabasco, and El Dorado Elixir (a Jackson family secret) were responsible? At least four people who visited Kenneth's Chili Wagon at the McKinley Summer Festival had supernatural visits from the grave later that night.

———⌇∽∽⌇———

Herb Nofsinger sat alone at his kitchen table at ten p.m. with a glass of cold whiskey in his hand, listening to June bugs whap against the screen of the back door. It was pitch black out, so black that the streetlight beyond his backyard almost seemed to have been swallowed whole by the darkness.

Herb felt strange and a little sad. That day he'd gone to the festival and wandered around looking for familiar faces. He'd seen a few—Dewey, who cashiered over at the Marathon, and A-Bomb, who'd helped him with the volunteer Gazebo construction project—but for the most part, McKinley had seemed overrun with people he didn't recognize. He'd chatted with Aaron Waggoner near the courthouse, then he'd gotten some chili and left.

The tick of the stove clock counted away the seconds, and in his heart, Herb felt a hard pull. His thoughts returned to Sarah, his wife, who'd died the year before. He wanted so badly to hear the sandpaper whisper of her slippers on the tile of the kitchen. He wanted to hear her sigh as she slid a bookmark into her novel just before going to bed.

When the handle on the door turned and Sarah came into the kitchen, Herb felt no fear—only a terrible and profound ache. He rose and looked into the watery blue eyes of his wife, at her small, sad smile, and then he took her into his arms and held her for a long time. "I love you and I miss you," Herb said, finally.

"I know," Sarah said. "Build something. Get out your tools, you'll feel better."

Herb began building a back porch the next day. The project would take him most of the fall to complete.

On the same night Herb Nofsinger saw his deceased wife, something strange and inexplicable happened to Andy Sumner, who was sitting up in bed reading *Mad Magazine*. His older brother Karl, two years dead from a factory accident, came into his room.

Karl stood by the door, bashfully looking at a poster Andy had taped up of a supermodel. Karl had always smiled a lot, and he was smiling now—his crooked teeth going in all directions, his eyes twinkling. Some people had thought Karl was retarded, but Karl had always just been nice. Too nice. Maybe Andy's big brother had been gullible, but he hadn't been dumb like everyone had thought.

Andy dropped his magazine and felt tears blur up his eyes so much that he couldn't even see his brother anymore. He wiped them away quickly, afraid that Karl would disappear.

"Hey, big brother," Andy said.

"Hey . . . hey." Karl said.

"What—What are you doing here?"

Andy's eyes traveled to Karl's hands, the hands that had gotten caught in the machine. They were fine.

"I used to say you drew funny," Karl said. The smile remained on his face, but Andy could tell that what he said was serious.

"Yeah, they were dumb pictures," Andy said.

"You haven't drawn in a while," Karl said.

"Yeah, I know. It's stupid, anyway."

"I shouldn't have told you they were dumb," Karl said. He looked away.

"Yeah?"

"They're good. They're real good," Karl said. "You should draw. A lot."

"Really? You think so?" Andy said. He stood up. He wanted to hug his brother. He wanted . . . something.

When he got close, however, Karl moved back.

"You're not dumb, either, Karl."

But Karl was already disappearing.

"I love you," Andy said. And then Karl was gone.

The same thing happened to David Kane; a presence from the afterlife visited him too. David didn't recognize this presence, though—not at first. When he left a friend's party that night, he found a middle-aged man sitting in the passenger seat of his old Trans Am.

David leapt out of the car when he realized this. Adrenaline flooded his circuitry, burning off most of his drunkenness.

"What the hell? What the hell?"

"Calm down," the old guy said. "I know your mother. I know *Jamie*."

David looked at the guy. He had a large gut on him, and there were dark circles under his eyes. He was wearing a baseball uniform that looked like it was from the '40s.

"Who are you?" David asked.

"Get in the car, I'll tell ya. You drive."

"I'm not going anywhere," David said.

The man sighed. He shook a cigarette out of a pack, lit it, and exhaled a cloud of smoke. "Son, we ain't got all night," he said.

"Are you kidnapping me? Is this some kind of extortion thing?"

The man looked at David. "You drive, we talk. You drive wherever you like."

David got in the car and started it.

"Who are you?" he asked.

"I'm dead," the man said.

David thought he might believe this.

He drove around for a few blocks. When they got close to his house, the man told him to pull over.

"I don't want nothing," the man said. "Except one thing. You got a choice: you play baseball, or you become an alcoholic ex-jock with a factory job. You become dead, like me."

"Who are you?" David said.

"Charlie," the man said. "Your mother's uncle. I died at thirty-three—my liver. I was a ballplayer. You'll notice I'm not wearing a Major League uniform."

The man tossed out his cigarette. A June bug flew into the car.

"Don't be like me," Charlie said. "Play ball."

Andrea Romito thought she might be better off dead.

She hated her life. She hated her gun-nut father. She hated how she was fat and flat-chested. She hated how boys ignored her, she hated most of the kids at her high school, and she hated the entire town of McKinley. About the only thing that made her forget these things was her cello playing; she was in orchestra at the high school.

She had gone to the Summer Fest in hopes of seeing one of the only people she liked—Brett Jones from school. Brett would be playing the band shell at one p.m. with his band, Rising Sons. In her mind, she had planned how it might go. She would stand at the front of the stage and make sure Brett knew she was there. After the set, she'd rush up and tell Brett what a great guitar player he was and everything.

When she'd gotten to the Fest and found Brett, he'd been unloading equipment from a van with Tim Janski and Jim Kohout. She'd been planning on going up to ask if they needed help, but then she'd seen Courtney Gray.

Courtney Gray had grabbed Brett around the waist and kissed his neck. Brett had turned around and grabbed her and practically sucked her face off.

Andrea hadn't been in the mood to see Rising Sons after that. She'd gone to another part of the Fest where she got some chili, sat on a park bench, and watched a couple play tennis.

Now at home in her room, Andrea thought she might just take a bottle of aspirin or throw herself into Dixmoor River.

These and other dark thoughts were swirling around inside her head when her dead sister, Lisa, came into the room. Lisa had been four years older than Andrea. She'd been killed by a drunk driver. Her hair was still long and straight, just like it had been on the day she'd died.

"No, Andrea," Lisa said. "Don't do it."

"Why not?" Andrea said. "There's nothing here for me."

"Maybe not here," Lisa said. "But, somewhere else."

"Where?"

"This is only one time in your life," Lisa said. "There will be other times. Better times. New places. New people. Wonderful experiences."

"How do you know that?"

"I just do," Lisa said. "Don't you want to find out what happens to you?"

"Not if it involves living here."

"You'll leave, one day," Lisa said.

"How?"

"Your music will carry you."

Kenneth Jackson, who made a modest but pleasant living selling hot dogs and chili from his storefront on Wildwood Street, did not sample his own cooking on the day of the McKinley Summer Fest. For this reason, he would never learn about the strange effect his chili had produced, and he would never know that he'd only been a few spoonfuls away from being visited by his deceased father, Earl.

Since Earl hadn't been known for his friendly disposition or tolerance, but rather for his abrasive, abusive, and unstable behavior, it was just as well this visit didn't take place.

Things were pretty good in Kenneth's life, all things considered.

He didn't need his father's advice.

One Shot

uring the drive up to Minneapolis, I'm trying to read this computer manual while Chris blasts Eminem. It's been four months of *this looks like a job for me,* and he's showing no sign of slowing down. There's some other song he absolutely loves, too: the one where Eminem promises *a good ass-fucking*! Chris turns up that lyric every time it comes around and laughs like it's the first time he's heard it.

We're going north from Chicago to visit our friend Sam, who has been living in Minneapolis for over a year. By all descriptions, he lives in a little hovel of an apartment and is scraping by while working at Walmart. The idea of our visit is to cheer Sam up or something, maybe talk him into moving back to Chicago. We're kinda worried about him.

The computer manual was written by someone with a nerdish sense of humor. There's a giddy geekiness to some parts of it that border on ultra-dweeb. Every so often I'll encounter a line like, "And you're done faster than you can say 'I think I'll go home early,'" or "Now you're on the road to *no extraneous data*!"

At first I was tempted to highlight these outbursts, if for no other reason than to amuse myself, but I knew I'd only be wasting time. I've been putting off reading this manual for months, and there's a site visit next week. One of the programmers (hopefully not the one who wrote the manual) is coming in from St. Louis, and I have to pretend I know something about this install. Blah blah blah—the point being, I have to get this fucker read, and it's not supposed to be fun.

Chris smokes a near-endless stream of cigarettes. When he bobs his head, like he's doing now to the rap beat, he looks sort of like a homeboy version of Matt Damon.

"Oh my God! Did you *see* that!?" Chris shouts. "I just saw two cows fucking!"

I turn quickly and look the direction Chris is pointing over my shoulder, and of course I missed it.

"They were fucking! I swear to God! One just dismounted as we were going past."

I shake my head and make a crib in this small neon-orange notebook.

"Man, that is so neat!" Chris says, looking at the notebook. "Is that your Harriet the Spy notebook?"

"Fuck you," I say. "Give me a cigarette."

I've been taking shit all the way up here with my obsessive compulsion to read ninety-eight pages of dry computer text. Clearly, Chris wants me to bug out to Eminem, or Crystal Method, or whatever he's got up next on his mod MP3 player with the laser-light-show frontpiece.

I haven't been to Minnesota for four years or so; the last time was a camping trip where I was ruthlessly attacked by mosquitoes. I remember the drive back, during which six or seven adjacent mosquito bites on my right kneecap joined to form one huge, throbbing mosquito bite. I vowed never to go back.

This time, there's no camping involved. It's just going to be me, Chris, and Sam hanging out at Sam's apartment—or at his real dad's house, where Sam has set up a makeshift recording studio in the living room while his parents are on vacation.

When we get to Dave, Minnesota, we drive around 3rd Street looking for Sam's place but can't find it. Finally, Chris pulls over at a liquor store and calls while I stock up on provisions of Bud.

Back in the car, a cold case on my lap, Chris tells me there's two Dave, Minnesotas. We're in the wrong one.

"No fucking way!" I grumble, fearing another two hours on the road with my new Budweisers turning to warm poison.

Chris laughs. "Just fuckin' with ya," he says, putting the car in gear. "It's a few blocks away."

I relax and take another look through the manual—I've only got forty pages to go.

Sam's place is somehow even more depressing than I imagined. It's a small one-bedroom where the kitchen and living room merge together. You can almost touch the refrigerator while you're sitting on the couch. It's a basement apartment that gets almost no outside light. There's a tiny window in the bathroom, Sam says; you can see sunlight through it, but only indirectly, from three to four in the afternoon.

"I'm usually asleep then," he says. "I work the night shift."

On the wall behind the TV, there's a huge green and red abstract painting. The green side is cool and smooth; the red side is garish and angry.

"Guess which side I did," Sam says.

"Red," Chris and I say together.

"No man, I did the green. My dad said the same thing—he thought I did the red. Jen did that. Check it out, doesn't it look crazy mad?"

We both nod our heads. Neither of us has ever met Jen, a girl Sam's been seeing for a few months. She's also out of town this weekend.

Sam tells us to relax. We kick back on the couch and open some beers, and Sam tells us what it's like to live in the outskirts of Minneapolis, alone in a town where he hardly knows anybody.

"It sucks, man," he says, "but I can afford it here. I get paid a little more for working the night shift stocking, but the job itself sucks. There's always some new company policy and shit. This year it's no overtime. They lied to us and told us it's because it's not fair to the other stores that don't get overtime. We know the profits are down. They're just too chickenshit to admit it's about money."

Sam's been playing his guitar, writing some new songs. He's been playing guitar and writing songs for a long time—nine or ten years. He's recording some this week while the house is free, trying to get a demo done on the four-track. You can tell he's determined by looking at his eyes. He's never giving up on this, no matter what poverty he has to endure, what embarrassment. He doesn't need anything else if he has his guitar.

Chris and I secretly hope that, one day, a record will release him from places he's stuck in—places like Walmart and cramped apartments in Dave, Minnesota.

"Know what the saying is out here?" Sam says. "'Holy Buckets.' That's it—'Holy Buckets.' Everybody says it. It's the fucking state phrase."

After a couple of beers, we decide to drive over to Sam's dad's place to jam a bit. Chris and I have lugged our guitars and amps in the trunk of Chris's Intrepid. If needed, I can resurrect some long-dormant drum skills on Sam's kit, or I can throw down some simple bass riffs on this used bass I've been messing around with for the last few months.

I'm ten years away from my last band, and I still sometimes wish I'd never quit. I was a competent drummer, by no means great, but I could have found another band if I'd bothered to try. At the time, I was so sick of the singers and the bullshit of being in a band that I sold the set and never thought I'd care.

Instead, I got out of college, got a "real job" that required 38-hour workweeks, a lockstep mentality, and the occasional reading of computer manuals.

Sam's dad is a train engineer who makes $80,000 a year, he tells us. There are pictures of trains on almost every wall. There's a pretty cool one of a train blasting through snow.

Almost any job is favorable compared to my job, so I'm instantly envious of this man's job. Really, I get that way when I hear about any job that allows one to afford a house and a family. I survive on pay that would hardly support a parakeet, much less a child.

We jam for a bit, letting Sam show us how to play his tunes, which are decent. Call it white man's blues: Beckish, but with more acid and cynicism.

Sam's dad has a framed copy of the Beatles' *White Album* on the wall. There are some scattered pictures of Lennon around as well. That's cool. Train conductor hanging on to some of his past; right on. But at the same time, in this climate-controlled house on the darkened, quiet street, the garage bin brimming with new toys and sports equipment, this life seems sort of closed down and cut off, like the end of the line.

I'm drunk now, I realize. I'm wondering again about what the end of my life will be like. Will I ever own a house? Have a wife? A family? Every year it's seemed less and less likely. Going without those things would be OK, but I have a dreaded image of myself living out my last years in an old folks' home in Uptown, watching a fuzzy TV and crapping my pants. I prefer to have my death come bounding—a lightning strike, a bus collision, a drive-by—anything but a slow, creeping death, much less one that I could be held responsible for by smoking too much, eating too much fat, etc. I don't mind dying, so long as it isn't *my* fault.

Each year, I imagine a way to escape: a move to California, to New York, to the country. I can never get the funds together. I can understand Sam moving here—at least he made a change. He gave himself a new environment. A new chance.

Sam tells us he's playing the local open mikes around town and that he's gotten some positive responses. The clubgoers seem to like him.

Problems of art don't concern Chris, a successful graphic designer. He can play guitar well enough, but his inclination to play in a band has never surpassed mine. We've both been there and done that, but with the difference that I've sometimes regretted it, while Chris doesn't seem to care.

"Let's go," Sam says, putting down his acoustic. "I hate hanging out here too long. I can't relax."

We break the stuff down and head back to Sam's place, where we drink underground for the next few hours. It's quiet here, much more so than in Chicago, and I feel vaguely threatened by the silence, like each passing second is another shovelful of dirt on my face. Eventually, Chris and I pass out on the couch and the floor respectively, while Sam goes to his room to continue working on some songs.

On Sunday, Chris and I plan on driving into Minneapolis proper and getting a hotel, doing the nightlife thing a bit. We want to bring Sam along, but in the morning Sam tells us he's feeling sick—he's been up all night, as is normal for him, working the late shift and everything (we were drinking, I realize, at the time he probably usually eats breakfast). He says he'll call us later.

Chris and I pull into the city and are amazed at how clean and still it is. It's like a model city more than an actual one—like one they would use in a movie, populate with actors, and blow apart. We check out a surgical-instruments museum, eat at a steak restaurant, and pass by the Mary Tyler Moore statue on the way to get some beer for the hotel.

We're saddened, but not really surprised, when Sam calls and tells us he's not up for the city. He's still feeling sick, etc. We put it down to debilitating paranoia, the fear of doing anything non-routine. We feel lousy about having only seen Sam for one night, but we've already got the hotel—there's nothing to do if he doesn't want to come out. We shrug it off and hit a local club where Prince supposedly used to play a lot.

We drink to excess again, but it's not much fun with just the two of us and the specter in our minds of Sam sitting in his tiny apartment, trying to write a song good enough to get him out of this place.

The next day, hungover, Chris and I are driving back, and I'm staring at the blue cover of the computer manual, which I can't seem to pick up. Finally, I kick it under the seat so I don't have to look at it anymore.

"Those were some good songs," I say to Chris as we pass farmhouses, silos, and cows not having sex.

"Yeah, they're almost there," he says, and then turns up this other Eminem song he can't seem to get enough of.

Bleedproof

She's in the Ranchero Strangiato late at night, enjoying a cigarette with her coffee, wearing a black T-shirt from the '70s that says "I Just Spent The Night With Muhammad Ali." The date for the Vegas bout is on the back. She's reading a book called *Success in the Business World*.

She sees me staring at the book, wondering.

"It's crap," she says, putting it down.

"Why are you reading it?"

"Because my father gave it to me."

"Is your father successful?"

"My father is dead."

Journal entry: There is something ancient in her eyes—death and strangulation.

We go see a junkie saxophonist who pays his rent in the room above by hooking his sax on Thursday nights. Offstage, he is a shambling, muttering old-man mess. Onstage, he's the oracle.

She waits tables and is working on a performance art piece in which a woman undergoes a species change to become a deer.

I almost don't make it in to work the next day. My lungs are Los Angeles on smog alert. My heart is a 1945 championship football. My nerves have more screwed-up connections than a Haitian phone company.

Journal entry: The graffiti in the bathroom was like Jung's unconscious.

Next date: a mainstream movie we both figure we'll hate. It's four hours long. The reel breaks halfway through. A horse disappears mid-leap.

"That was enough," she says, while someone unseen scrambles to tape the celluloid back together. "Let's go for coffee."

We take a cab to the Strangiato. On the way, there are ice slicks and dangerous speeds. We almost hit a BMW. At the cafe, I give the driver an extra five bucks for not killing us.

At the end of the counter a man is telling another: "Fuck relax! I haven't relaxed since 'Nam!"

The cook's eyes are chemical, fires dancing in a gale, threatening to extinguish at any second.

Later, in bed, after sex, I tell her she is a beautiful mystery.

She says: "My life is *Good Times* without J. J."

Journal entry: I am as much for World War III as against it.

We are traveling near San Francisco. She has a box of fortune cookies open on her lap; she's cracking them open and reading the forgettable wisdom before tossing the white paper, like doomed sperm, out the window.

We are looking for a motel. Her rule is that we have to find the one with the dumbest name. We settle on the Islander, which has a giant rainbow fish out front. Inside the room it is 1963. Ice buckets, VO5 hair gel, and Vantage cigarettes.

"I love it," she says, hopping on the too-solid mattress.

I turn the Magnavox to the weather. America is shown tie-dyed in reds, blues, greens, and yellows. Systems move across her face. A man in a tight suit tries to explain.

"I want to call my first book *The Nocturnal Scream of the Ape*," she says. "New York will understand."

At the birthplace of John Wayne, my camera dies. She laughs beside the bust of the Duke, stoned. "Maybe this is just something to take home in your mind."

We move in together, eating dinner in near-total darkness. She says she hates the sight of food.

She has been talking for weeks now about her need to hemorrhage.

"I want ulcers," she says. "I want to bleed."

"You do bleed."

"I want to bleed *more*."

I catch her cutting her palms with a razor one night while she's listening to talk radio.

Journal entry: Some relationships are like watching a flower flourish and die in elapsed time.

We are bitter about our living conditions. Poor, the both of us. "I just want an uncrooked floor and a decent stove, not owned by Satan, in a neighborhood where I won't get shot at. Is that too much to ask?"

I have always but a few dollars in my checking account, which I monitor obsessively, like the vital signs of a dying patient.

She has an idea for money: Think Twice Abortion Cards. She wants to market this to Hallmark.

A video concept: *Psych Majors Gone Wild.*

She wants a new holiday: Punch an Asshole in the Mouth Day. Have Anonymous Sex with a Stranger Day. I am almost inclined.

She is drawing again, sending me on errands to buy pads of expensive Paris Bleedproof, furrowing the surface with crow quills and singeing designs with a Bic.

From a crack-addicted neighbor, she buys a dog we cannot afford for nine dollars.

Journal entry: Life is not unlike crouching in a ditch while mortar shells explode around you.

The dog dies of an unknown disease. She attempts to bury it and can't get the shovel into the earth. She places the dog in a garbage bag and throws it into the river. Instead of sinking, it floats toward the water filtration plant.

"I can't even bury a dog right," she says, tears streaking down her face.

She's trying to sell things to pawn shops. Unreasonable things: rusty guitar strings, a broken humidifier, a protractor from high school, rationalizing that she has no use for them. Not considering why others would.

"I'll bring down this pig system if it kills me!" she says, more and more.

The night before her species change she collapses, overmedicated, in an alley. The cops are not kind.

"What's the story, Hemingway? This chick your girlfriend?"

A light snow is starting to fall.

With any luck, it will cover everything.

Arrested Development

S ometimes I see him at night, in dreams, standing in the yellow light of his bedroom window.

In these dreams, he's not dead. He's not a cadaver hanging from the rafters of a garage in Springfield, Illinois.

In these dreams, he's his favorite football player, Tony Dorsett of the Dallas Cowboys, my adversary in backyard games of football.

He's my fellow junior arsonist, building small fires to deform plastic cowboys and infantrymen.

He's the bastard son of a Vietnamese woman and an American GI. He was born in 1969 and brought to the states by an Army priest, adopted by a Catholic family, and placed in the custody of wrist-whacking nuns.

He is not the ultimate misfit who was kicked out of his home at eighteen, not the depressive twenty-year-old alcoholic father of a child he will never know.

This is before all that. In my dreams, he is my best friend from ages 6 to 12 who lived kitty-corner from me.

He is Professor Plum to my Colonel Mustard.

The Monopoly Top Hat to my Shoe.

He is not yet a dropout kicking about town with denim-wearing kids much younger than himself, a case of arrested development.

He is not yet the displaced young man my horrified mother saw begging for change in front of our local Ace Hardware.

He is, instead, the child who used to come to our house for dinner, eagerly eating up plates of mostaccioli.

Right now, as I look up at that window, he is the kid who had to take piano lessons against his will. The one who forgot his workbook at school a lot. The one who shared the discovery of women between the pages of a rain-soaked *Playboy*.

He is the Imperial TIE Fighter to my Rebel X-Wing.

Conan to my Wolverine.

He is a haunted-house designer, hedge jumper, and dirt-bike explorer.

Ponch to my John.

Rocky to my Mickey.

Han to my Luke.

I am not reading about his death in the local paper we once delivered. Instead, we are fishing in his father's rowboat in Michigan, our feet covered in perch.

He is not a wasted body swinging from a beam.

He is also definitely not a corpse laid out in the basement of the same funeral home we used to race by, as kids, on our way to the candy store to exchange returnable Pepsi bottles for Snickers, Twizzlers, and Volcano Rocks.

He cannot be the focal point of a funeral service I am too chickenshit to attend.

No, right now he is secretly alive, hidden away from the world in a locked room of his parents' house with a Mickey Mouse poster on the wall.

He is the friend who swore we'd be together forever, eventually living with our wives in side-by-side log cabins in Alaska.

Self-sufficient.

Living off the land.

Ourselves; all we'd ever need.

The Blue Pig

You could always tell it was Fledge because, no matter what kind of beat-up car he drove, it always had the same bumper sticker on it: *Burt Reynolds Is Driving This Car*. And you could always tell it was Officer Lofredo because of the tight-assed way of walking he had, the way he tended to tilt forward, hitching up his police utility belt and cracking his neck as he went about his daily routine of trying to sniff out some crime.

If you'd ever been to a Fledge party, you'd have seen the two of them butt heads; it had happened numerous times. Usually it would be at the height of a Friday or Saturday night. Led Zeppelin would be blasting out of Fledge's screenless windows; people would be doing coke off Thin Lizzy mirrors in the bedroom; the backyard would be overcrowded with every beer-drinking badass and gearhead in DuPage County. The whole block would smell like bong hit. Lofredo would pull up with his gumballs flashing and wait a few minutes before getting out of the cruiser and pounding on the door, effectively allowing the partiers the opportunity to squash joints and send any minors to the basement laundry room.

Fledge would be summoned, and he would steam up to the door and squeeze onto the porch. "What's up . . . *Dick*?" he'd say.

This was Officer *Richard* Lofredo, of course.

Lofredo would give his best menacing stare, crack his neck a couple of times, and say, "Turn it down, Fledge, we got a noise complaint."

"What? They don't like Led Zeppelin?" Fledge would say. (He'd always change the name of the band to match whatever was currently blasting out of the windows.)

"Time to come up with a new comeback, Fledge," Lofredo would say, and Fledge would just smirk at him.

"Last warning. Turn it down, and get those minors home. It's past curfew."

Fledge would go back in and stop the music player for five minutes while he located a certain album—David Peel and the Lower East Side Band's *The American Revolution*—and then he would put it on and play the early seventies cop-hater anthem "Oink, Oink" at fifty decibels.

It wasn't uncommon for Lofredo (or some other hapless officer) to return and repeat the warning, but by that time the party would usually be winding down anyway. Even if Fledge were to continue to ignore the warnings, it was unlikely that anything as serious as an arrest would happen. Though Fledge was one of Weston's premier fuck-ups, he had diplomatic immunity: his father was the brother of the mayor of Weston. Members of the Zajdel family were generally not hauled off to jail.

Most of the time, the almost-weekly showdowns between Fledge and Officer Lofredo were amicable. Both players were aware of their roles—of what they could and could not get away with. Still, the complaints were real, and it was not a matter that could just be brushed aside. Lofredo had visited the front door of Fledge's small clapboard home many times over the years, and he'd grown weary of having his hands tied when it came to this frizzy-haired punk.

One Saturday night, it came to pass that Officer Lofredo appeared yet again on the doorstep of Fledge Zajdel, and that night just happened to be the eve of Fledge's thirtieth birthday. It was a rowdier night than usual on the cusp of this important milestone, and Fledge was correspondingly wasted when he lunged toward the door where Lofredo stood waiting for him.

"What's up, Officer Lofucko?" Fledge asked.

Lofredo's usual entreaties about turning the music down and getting the minors out were dutifully repeated. This time, however, they met with the suggestion from Fledge that the good officer go fuck himself.

Lofredo, for his part, kept his cool. As an officer, this was expected of him, even required. Besides, he had too much wrapped up in his career—a mortgage to pay off, a car payment for a new Monte Carlo, a baby girl on the way—to do something stupid like haul off on this buckethead. Instead, Lofredo suggested that he and Fledge meet someplace and settle this rivalry like men.

Normally, Fledge would not have been enticed; however, he had located the bottom of at least twenty cans of Old Style that evening and was therefore not in the best of judgment states. While he stood there trying to process a good comeback, his new girlfriend, Christine, a petite, sharp-tongued creature, spoke for him.

"Sure, he'll do it," she said to Lofredo. "He'll kick your motherfucking ass, too!"

If there was any sliver of fear in Fledge, it was hard to make out within the bleary and loose expression he wore.

"Hellfire!" he said, and belched.

"How about it, Fledge?" Lofredo asked. "Me and you, *mano a mano*? I'll even give you a month to get your worthless ass into shape."

"Fledge'll be there," Christine said, spattering saliva on Lofredo's face. "Fuckin' A right!"

And so it was decided that a duel should take place a month hence.

Waking up the following morning, Fledge felt poisoned. His mouth tasted like dragon shit. As he stumbled towards the bathroom seeking the relief of Ibuprofen, weird memories and dreams slid through the ooze of his mind. He kept trying to get to something. Something had happened the night before. He looked at his fingers. They were all there. No major cuts were in evidence; that was good.

Then he remembered Lofredo.

"Lofucko" he said, chuckling at the memory. But a second later he was still. He recalled Lofredo's fight challenge. Then, worse, he recalled the rumor of the challenge spreading through the party, with everyone encouraging Fledge to send Lofredo to the sweet hereafter.

"Christ," Fledge said, examining his pale, slack face in the mirror. He gulped down two pain relievers. To refuse to fight was not an option. He was an icon; he couldn't let his weekend warriors down. To chicken out would result in a loss of respect. Worse, they might start buying weed from someone else.

"Fuck, fuck, *fuck*."

He lifted his arms and attempted to flex his muscles. His biceps were like tubes of jelly. They were muppet arms.

As the day wore on and Fledge's hangover burned off, he found himself forced to accept that the fight was inevitable. He had vainly hoped that the challenge would be forgotten—if not by Lofredo, then at least by the partygoers—but no sooner had Fledge slumped onto the couch to watch the Sox game than the phone starting ringing as various friends called to wish him luck and offer their support.

"Who was that?" Christine asked, when Fledge hung up the phone.

"That was Woogie. He says he's got gallons of this bulk-up shake stuff in his garage. He's gonna bring some over to help me gain a few pounds."

Ken Dynacko, probably one of the toughest sons-of-bitches west of Cook County, told Fledge he was welcome to come over to weight-train in his basement.

"I'll turn you into a monster, dude," he said. "One month."

When Fledge got a third call from Kurt Gozdel, who said he'd be willing to show Fledge some martial-arts moves, it depressed him even further. Clearly, all of his friends thought he was going to get his ass kicked.

The next several weeks were a whirlwind of physical activity that Fledge hadn't experienced since seventh-grade gym class. He cut back on his Marlboro reds, ate high-protein meals at every opportunity, and gulped shake after shake of powdery, expired Mota Fuel. For extra inspiration, he put together a tape showing the sequences from *An Officer and a Gentleman, Rocky I,* and *Stripes* where Gere, Stallone, and Murray, respectively, realize what physical wrecks they are and vow to do something about it.

If there was a kind of solidarity among the skids of Weston, there was a similar bond among the police over at the station. News of the fight was kept hush-hush from administration, but all the regular cops had the date marked on their calendars and looked forward to watching Lofredo vanquish Fledge in front of his stoner pals. But by week three of his training, Fledge was feeling more confident about his chances. Endless coaching from Dynacko and Gozdel had actually brought about some results, though Fledge still winded easy and sometimes broke down in coughing fits when he exerted too much energy.

On the day of the fight, stoners trailed from all over to Saint Rita's parking lot as if for a Grateful Dead concert. On the other side of the lot, cops and friends of cops parked their gleaming SUVs and pickup trucks. Lofredo emerged from the back of a minivan that was decorated on the side with a banner that read "THE BLUE PIG." Fledge emerged from a van with a wizard painted on the side wearing a shiny gold cape; someone had written "OLD STYLE" over it. The crowd formed behind the church on a patch of grass that was secluded by trees. The referee for the match was Father Brown, a rum-nosed pastor who had boxed semiprofessionally back in the day.

Father Brown explained the rules to the fighters and then backed into the circle of bystanders, where he hit a disconnected school firebell with the end of a metal crucifix. The opponents stalked toward each other while their support crews yelled encouraging remarks from the sidelines.

"Get him, Fledge!"

"Smoke the doper, Lofredo! Smoke him!"

Once he was on the grassy ring, Fledge forgot nearly everything he'd been taught over the past several weeks. He opened up on Lofredo quickly and left himself unprotected. Lofredo dodged some ineffectual swings easily and then closed in on him. Above the crowd's shouting, Fledge could hear Christine screeching out in her high-pitched, nasal whine: "Cream him, Fledge! *Cream* him!"

Actually, Fledge had already known it was over the second he'd set foot into that churchyard. You can't make up for fifteen years of hard partying in one month. He was outmatched. He had already begun to wheeze. Blindly, he rushed in and attempted an unwise cross punch, which Lofredo easily blocked and used as an opportunity to send a rocket at Fledge's face. To onlookers it appeared as if Fledge's circuitry had been cut off. His knees buckled, his torso went limp, and he flopped to the grass like a puppet severed from its strings. He lay motionless just long enough for the assembly to consider what a world without Fledge would be like. Then, he moaned and his legs pulled up, and it became clear that he was not dead—only defeated.

"Shit, man, I told you to keep your fists up. Your head is the meat, your hands are the bread. Sandwich, man! *Sandwich*!"

Dynacko's comments were barely heard, however. Fledge was carried off into the van while Lofredo basked in his win, high-fiving his buddies, until all insults had been traded by each side and the crowd finally dispersed.

Lofredo had probably presumed that a win in this match would result in a new respect for his person and the law, and, for the next three weeks while Fledge healed, Lofredo was given no cause to visit the Zajdel residence to respond to a noise complaint. Various officers enjoyed reminding any burnout wastelifes they happened to pull over for traffic infractions about the resounding defeat of their "Dope King" and generally seemed to be under the impression that justice had prevailed.

Before long, however, Fledge felt compelled to shed his low profile, and he threw another rager. This time, it was an event that he called "The Summer's Almost Gone Party." Windows were opened on the top floor of his home as various partygoers stripped down to their underwear and jumped into the above-ground pool in the backyard. A local Black Sabbath cover band was mid-set, and Fledge was standing on a ladder in the backyard rocking to "Sweet Leaf," his arms extended in a fringe-flapping Ozzy/Nixon peace wave, when Lofredo showed up to enforce the right of non-Sabbath-lovers to have their peace and quiet.

When he was informed of the officer's arrival, Fledge climbed off the ladder and put down his cup of beer. Christine followed at his heels, but this time he told her to stay back. He went through the house to the front door and stepped onto the stoop.

"Hi, Fledge," Lofredo said.

"Officer," Fledge said.

"How's the face?"

"Not as ugly as yours."

Lofredo smiled.

"I can work on it some more if you like."

Attracted by the flashing lights, some people crept from the sides of the house to see what was going on. Fledge ordered them to the back-yard.

"Let's turn it down, huh, Fledge? Tell that band to pack it up now."

"I'd be delighted to," Fledge said.

Lofredo narrowed his fish eyes at Fledge, trying to read him.

"Anything else?" Fledge said.

"Just do it," Lofredo said. He went back to his cruiser.

Fledge told the band to call it a night.

There were sounds of surprise and general dismay as some of the partygoers grumbled that Fledge had gone soft, that he was now Lof-redo's toady. Ignoring these remarks, Fledge returned to the house and started fitting speakers into the windows facing the street. He then lo-cated his David Peel album and put "Onk, Oink" on as loud as it could go. He played it repeatedly until the seal on his diplomatic immunity was finally broken and Lofredo returned and arrested him.

Both parties declared victory.

About the Author

J ohn H. Matthews' fiction has appeared in anthologies and several literary magazines. He lives near Chicago with his lovely wife Rachel and their American bulldog. This is where he writes, plays bass guitar and goes fishing whenever possible.

Acknowledgments

'd like to thank (in alphabetical order) the following people, who gave me inspiration, assistance, encouragement or beer money during the writing of this collection: David Barringer, Setalo Csaba, Blair Henkle, Terry Jacobus, Tom Klaeren, Frank Marcopolos, Mike & Becca Matthews, Dehlia McCobb, Martin Northway, Anthony Oltean, Doug & Kirsten Pagacz, Phyllis Pagacz, Richard A. Reiter, and of course, my family.